The
Inventors
Daryl Li

• CONTENTS •

Come back!
Even as a shadow,
even as a dream.

Herakles

THE
PHYSICS OF MEMORY
)

■ Entanglements

2019

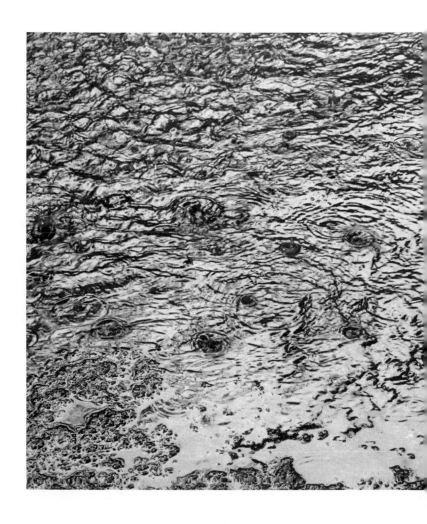

I

There were no seats and we all ate standing. The tables were spare, basically bar tables with black cloths draped over them. We were separated from friends and grouped into three clusters with strangers. While waiting for things to get started, we passed paper serviettes around almost as a courteous ice-breaking ritual.

The event, a collaboration between chef Ming Tan and artist Debbie Ding which married food and art, was titled *SAD: The Last Meal*. It sought to imagine the Singapore food culture of the future, as a way of complicating the rather straightforward and romantic idea of nostalgia that had been circulating in public discourse. The description intrigued me, and I was happy to sign up for anything even mildly subversive, and so I bought my ticket without a second thought. I hadn't read the description too closely. It was unlike anything else that I had attended before so, uncertain of exactly what to expect, I brought a friend along for safety.

When we got to the doors, however, our names were checked against a list, and we were each assigned to a number corresponding to one of three groups. And so, all rather unceremoniously, we were split up. I began to feel a tinge of regret. I went into the room and was directed to Group 1's cluster of tables. I stood alone in a corner of the space, which was just about large enough to house maybe 40 people. There was an eye-catching display of two or three dozen soft toys suspended from the ceiling, though it was only much later—a few days later, in fact—that I learnt that that while thematically related, that exhibit was not part of the same event.

Certain that spending the entire evening forcibly separated from my companion and without anyone else to talk to would be unbearable, I resolved to participate to the best of my ability. Besides, short of walking away, what else could I have done? There was a sense that this wasn't what I had paid for, and yet, in the worlds of art and fine dining, it can sometimes be hard to tell. I recognised that my discomfort was an intended effect. Still, as a nervous sort, the cloudiness of such social encounters—the rush of strange faces, the chorus of unfamiliar voices, the uncertainty of each utterance, the rehearsed niceties—has never been kind to me. As I watched the people filtering in, I still had no clue what the night had in store for me. Suspecting that they were as confused as I was, I panned my gaze around, looking for someone to meet it, hoping to start some conversation. Beside me was a flat-screen TV, about the size of a classroom desk, and a boy, at most 15. He would spend the evening eating quickly, fidgeting about, and refusing eye contact with anyone else. It wasn't hard to guess that he had been dragged to the event by his parents and really wasn't in much of a mood to talk. Nevertheless, I tried my best, but he was able to escape my most valiant attempts to make eye contact.

Hello, a voice said just then. An enormous wave of relief washed over me. I turned and was relieved to see a friendly face. She was maybe 26 or 28, had long, straight hair, a watch around her right wrist, and shoes with reflective lining. She looked just as confused about what she was doing there.

Hello, I said back. In the moment, I thought about saying more, like a simple how are you to follow up the initial greeting, but I thought better of it. It has always confused me. Why do we ask how are you and what's up when there can be no satisfactory answer? Is it a way to signal courtesy, an evidently false I-care-about-you? Are they beginnings of stories that we know we will never be able to properly tell? At best these are frivolous courtesies, and at worst, they suggest a presumption, that somehow, we'll be able to know something—anything. In Chinese, we say: 吃飽了嗎?(Have you eaten?) There is something charmingly grounded about the greeting, less existential, less ambitious, more to-the-point, planted firmly in the discourse of food and subsistence, the basic condition of existing. Perhaps that question is fairer, something that points towards our bodily machinery without overreaching, without any suggestion of being able to reach for a deeper truth.

Do you know what this is all about? she said.

I know a little bit, I said, the lack of confidence stemming from my surprise at how the whole event was playing out. I looked up the webpage and read to her part of the description.

She nodded and said: A friend brought me here.

I see.

And you?

Uhh, I brought a friend here, I said, sheepish.

The event got under way after a quick introduction from the two creators. The food was prepared in the same space, with the kitchen set up behind folding screens. Every so often, I would peek through the gaps, hoping to see what was in store for us. I never succeeded, mainly because I felt guilty as soon as I caught the slightest glimpse of it, as though I was some kind of cooking voyeur. I was nervous, partly in anticipation of the food that would come, and partly because I felt as though I was dishonestly prying into some secret.

The first course was a take on chicken rice, often described as Singapore's national dish. It was served in the familiar Styrofoam boxes that we'd find in hawker centres. A fizz of anticipation surfaced in me—didn't know what I would find. The squeak of Styrofoam echoed through the room. I looked into the box to find a rice cake in the shape of a flying saucer, a fine powder the colour of chilli sauce, a paste that smelled of garlic and ginger, and dark soy sauce.

There was just enough that the original dish would register, but it also felt as if they were going for the shock, a violence towards something so familiar, so sacred that it was clearly intended to set the tone. I looked to my left and she seemed to pause momentarily. I looked to my right and the young boy was already digging in as though he couldn't wait for all of this to be over. The rice equivalent felt cold to the touch, and in terms of texture, it was somewhat like a ketupat, but finer, and a little more congealed. While I wasn't all that taken with it, the chilli sauce powder was addictive, and I've always been something of a soy sauce enthusiast. But those were condiments. I began seriously contemplating if I would still be hungry by the end of the event.

Maybe we'll all have to go for McDonald's after this, she

quipped. While I don't think anyone went into the event expecting gastronomic indulgence, as a whole, the dish was brazenly unsatisfying. But that was the point of the course, if not the entire event—absence. In imagining the food of the future, it also imagined a future without the food of today. It imagined a time in which the present moment was no longer within reach. This was reinforced by the images on the screens, which showed a chef preparing each of these dishes in their original form, reminding participants of the dish that they were supposed to have, now extruded through the pixels, concept, and light—ideas haunted by the lack of their material qualities, ghosts.

These images offered failed promises. They reminded us of the absences in front of us. As image, they were illusions, tricks of light. And rather than simple images of said dish, they were videos of their preparation, underlining the fleeting nature of food and food culture. After all, like all culture, food is performance, expression, memory, decay,

the blooming of the flower,

the deaths of stars.

II

The unnerving sense of expectation clung exasperatingly to proceedings. Each moment of awkward silence felt like a test. She smiled and tried to make conversation again. I played my part, but my mind was distracted. I knew this was a lost cause. We would never meet again after the evening. My mind drifted to potentialities, across many possible, many imagined futures. I wondered if we would become friends, unlikely as it seemed. No, in fact, I knew that it was impossible. We would soon go our separate ways, never to meet again. There was nothing to read here, no predictable futures, no possible hopes. The best I could hope for was the fantasy of parallel universes, of different moments, of different coincidences.

Several years ago, knowing almost nothing about Chinese theatre— or indeed, theatre in general—I was urgently drawn to a play that was to be a part of the annual Chinese arts festival for reasons I didn't quite understand. I was a different person then. I had barely emerged from my teenage years. I was confused about my future. I still had all my teeth. I thought I was in love.

We were university classmates. One day after class I caught up to her in the lift, and we exchanged awkward greetings. I had been planning to ask her if she wanted to catch the show together. Ironically, something about being in the lift with a group of strangers was oddly comforting to me. Perhaps it was the knowledge that I would never have to worry about these folks ever knowing who I was.

As I stood in the lift panicking, unsure of what I was even doing, I found that even as I opened my mouth to speak, the words wouldn't come. I floundered. My pulse rose. I began to sweat. No, I was already sweating because I had run to catch the lift, but the situation ensured that I would only continue to do so. I realised that I had grown a bit breathless as well. It was far from the first time that my body had betrayed me, but I also knew that I was performing my discomfort, in the hopes that she would notice. There was an echo of Roland Barthes's *A Lover's Discourse*, in which he describes a notion of performative distress. I had always found striking that such self-awareness would change the meaning of the sign. This discomfort would no longer—could no longer—be sincere. Barthes explains that the motto *larvatus prodeo*, from Descartes, is to advance pointing to one's mask. This motto, no matter the accuracy of his interpretation, describes an ironic consciousness at the heart of his work. It seemed fitting that I had asked her to watch a play.

I had brought along a prop, a brochure that quickly summarised that I was asking her without me having to resort to my nervous Mandarin. I looked at the brochure. The play was directed by Tian Qin Xin and adapted from an Eileen Chang novella called《紅玫瑰與白玫瑰》(*Red Rose, White Rose*). Chang rose to prominence during the rise of modern Shanghai and the accompanying cultural explosion of the era. She wrote her first novel at the age of 12. Later in her life, she also worked as a researcher and a translator. Chang's writing focuses on the experience of women, the subversion of nationalistic narratives, and the tensions and contradictions emerging in a traditional Chinese society in its encounter with modernity. Her work and life are an important part of modern Chinese literary culture.

I knew that the other passengers in the lift had absolutely no interest in whatever was unfolding, or Eileen Chang and her remarkable literary output, for that matter. In my mind's eye, I could see myself taking two different paths—to keep quiet and let the moment pass, or to ask the question—as though they were my two selves. Terrified, I chose the latter, and instantaneously, the other path, the other me grew out of reach. There was a surge of despair, which I struggled against ineffectually, as though I had chosen to foolishly position myself against the onrushing tide.

As all this drama swirled in my mind and I became engrossed in this ghastly self-absorption, she simply said yes. She said it so quickly that I thought I had imagined it. The story you have in your head never really matches any physical reality. This story in your head is your other world, your other life, your other body. One can inform the other, can enrich the other, but they can also be mutually destructive.

As soon as I got home, I purchased the tickets.

As these things tend to go, I remember everything that was bad about the day. The curry we had for dinner was absolutely mediocre, and the dinner conversation had a stop-start rhythm to it that was unnatural, jarring. (It is my one great talent.) She told me that she had come to this show with me instead of with her best friend at the time, and so I felt especially responsible for ensuring that she had a decent night out. I was doing a terrible job.

We walked over to the Esplanade after dinner. I remember it being quite cold that evening. Along the way, we did our best to sustain the illusion of conversation, keen to reach the point in the evening when we could let the show take over.

Perhaps betraying my lack of theatre-going experience, the large crowd outside the venue amazed me. In retrospect, it should hardly have been surprising. Tian Qin Xin was a director of some renown, and it starred well-known thespians Qin Hailu and Gao Hu. I suppose it was the atmosphere that surprised me, so different from going to, say, the movies here in Singapore. It felt grand, weighty, convivial, alive.

The novella *Red Rose, White Rose* is about Zhenbao, an average man caught between a good wife and a passionate mistress, the white and red roses respectively. The theatre production homed in on the theme of choice, of the gripping premise of taking one different turn and living a wholly different life. Zhenbao was portrayed by two actors, emphasising the duality of his life, and a large part of the show had these two actors humorously debating the choices he could, should, and would have made. There was a transparency to the play: the walls and doors were see-through; the two Zhenbaos had a view of the whole stage, of all goings-on, all internal lives, and effectively, an omniscient view of time; and the fog that separated audience and performance was pierced from the start. This was in service of the play's thematic concerns. It was about the branches of our paths in life that we could never see, and through the magic of theatre, it made those paths visible, legible. Of course, no one can rewind to any moment, no one can precisely see the consequences of any decision. That would dilute time and agency. Besides, things tend not to lead so neatly from cause to effect, every choice a pebble, a bud, every moment a ripple, a bloom.

This fantasy draws on a particular human fallacy. We imagine futures and prescribe for ourselves outcomes. We enjoy the sense of knowing, the power of certainty. There is an attraction to the cause-and-effect illusion, that things happen for discernible reasons. For a long time, I could not explain why I was disturbed by the argument that if a person works hard for something, they will reap the rewards. And if they fail, it's because they didn't put in the work—a type of perverted narrative of hope. Things happen for a reason, sure, or for a multitude of reasons, but in presuming total explicability, we presume to control the narrative. It blinds us to the whimsicality, unpredictability, surprise, the elements of performance, the possibilities of chance. It prescribes the future ahead of time.

I've often wondered if Eileen Chang's own life inspired *Red Rose, White Rose* directly. She had a complicated romantic life, and some of her other work would be easily classified as *roman a clef.* I wondered if it was a specific regret or a particular helplessness that she was channelling. Regret, in particular, fascinated me. I didn't manage to put it into words at the time, but years later, I would realise that regret thrives on the idea that there is a traceable path from our choices to the outcomes, that there is no such thing as chaos. I shouldn't have done that, we say, as if we could have known, as if implying that the future has already been written. It is only with the transition from uncertainty to destiny that regret achieves its full expression.

It is 2015 when Simon Jarrett makes an accidental journey across decades by way of a brain scan. Trapped in a research facility, Simon survives with the help of Catherine Chun, who gives him suggestions and advice remotely as he navigates obstacle after obstacle.

As I embark on a frightening odyssey in the horror-themed video game *Soma*, I take control of the Frankenstein's monster formed by the combination of this 2015 brain scan and an advanced biomechanical body. I am the cutting edge of technology. I am wondrous. I am grotesque.

The bulk of the game takes place in the far future, almost a century after Simon's brain patterns and memories have been copied, and a year after a catastrophic comet impact that leaves the remnants of humankind struggling to get by. As I make my way through obstacle after obstacle, hazard after hazard, trying my best to answer the questions the game poses to me, the central tension of the game becomes rendered with increasing clarity.

One of the things that Catherine asks him to do is to transfer his brain scan—his consciousness—from body to body. This occurs by copying the brain scan into the target body, and then destroying the originating one. In the end, Simon accomplishes his goal and catapults his way to a life away from this dying planet, but in doing so, is unable to delete the copy that is left behind—the copy that is not destroyed, the copy that lost the coin toss.

I remember finding the story a little tired, but it was effective nonetheless. Despite knowing early on exactly where the story was heading, it remained unnerving throughout. There was also something about seeing it through myself as a player that made it doubly awful to experience. Perhaps it resonated with my discomfort with such fictive tropes of multiplicity, the notion of the multiplied self, made possible with tropes such as time travel, the technological translation of memory, and human cloning.

One, of course, gets left behind. One leaves, and one gets left behind, a split in the universe, a crack in time.

My exposure to theatre productions at the time was limited, which may explain why I found the play astounding. It thrived on its nature as theatrical construct, on the alchemical engagement of the audience through the fourth wall, the flow of irretrievable instants. It wore a certain irony on its sleeve, an irony that I would later strive failingly to attain in my own work, Barthes's *larvatus prodeo*, Vila-Matas when he describes the "conscience that would be nothing without irony"[1], something self-aware and performative, yet not self-indulgent, not smug.

I went back to the theatre time and time again, always eager for new experiences, but also in search of glimpses of what I knew I would never find again, the echoes of a story. All things considered, it was a mediocre date with a brilliant play. There was too much to remember. The sounds of the actors' voices, the particular glow from the screens displaying the surtitles, the way she looked, the things we spoke about, the things we didn't, my particular nervousness. I think it was only in that moment that I understood theatre. We had all congregated—performers, producers, audience members—in a specific and unique configuration of the universe, under one agreement in order to engineer one moment. The moment passed, and we were no longer capable of accessing it. This is true of all moments, but performance—with its tools of liveness, repetition with difference, time-decay—was the means by which it was emphasised.

It was a foolish enterprise, more like peering through a veil in search of cinders that had bloomed so briefly. That more Chinese theatre would conjure the same experiences or feelings was the flimsiest of promises. The actors were different, the plays were different, and each show was also marked by her absence—and *my* absence, the me that could no longer be recovered, the one whom I am a copy of.

Over time, I came to realise that I was totally responsible for ruining my date at the theatre. I had spent so much time engineering its outcome that it had obscured how the encounter—the performance of it—was the most precious. I regretted the way things had turned out, the things I felt I didn't say, the things I felt I should have said—a common refrain—but also the way I had spent so much energy worrying and imagining the outcomes instead of being in it, prescribing, *pre*-scribing, writing ahead of time, searching for the right set of answers. I didn't understand then that things could never have been predictable or that they would fit within an idealised narrative. Perhaps, fearful of failure, I had chosen to embarrass myself from the start, in pursuit of the dull pain of regret.

As time passed, my confidence in the things I could remember dwindled, and in muted desperation, I turned it into stories, turned it into writing, to keep the memory alive. Yet the more I did so, the more I obscured the moment. I realised that the memory had solidified into something else, a vapid coagulation, unbearable in its stability.

As I continued in this fruitless pursuit, my quest for ever-diminishing returns, I learnt it is not simply that the river always runs, but that we too are the river, never running through the same world twice. I kept looking, and yet the memory remained the same in my mind, impervious to decay, distilled into the things we chose to say, the thoughts I thought I had, the beginning, middle, and end, the stories we tell ourselves, believing that they live up to this fantasy, but no

> nothing except

> letters in

calcified time

III

The Last Meal was a four-course, so after the chicken rice, there was carrot cake, laksa, and douhua. Inevitably, a curation of the representative dishes of a country was bound to perform some mythologisation. *The Last Meal* played on expectations and narratives of a national food culture. In doing so, it underlined how our stories serve to honour, to commemorate, to celebrate, but also unavoidably render violence to the very things that they remember.

The laksa turned out to be my favourite. It was probably everyone's favourite. By this point, I had also stopped worrying about what was in store for me and started really enjoying the event. The highly conceptual dishes were certainly succeeding in prompting thoughts and questions in me.

Laksa is said to be a national dish, perhaps because of the convenient symbolism that it offers. The narrative is attractive—a dish borne from the melding of different food cultures at an idealised crossroads. On the screens, this blending of cultures was given expression vibrantly, through a performance that enacted the combination of ingredients and methods that came together not in the melting pot of lore, but a bowl of rice noodles that was simultaneously a mass of citations that referenced histories and lineages, the realised expression of memories and flavour combinations.

The laksa in *The Last Meal* was presented with a twist, taking the form of a rice cereal with a powdered soup base mixed in— laksa by way of American breakfast food and instant noodles. We tried it dry first, and then the chef came by with a pot of hot water, as though we were making cup noodles. It was a citation of citations. There was something especially delightful about the two-part presentation, and its form as a snack food and resemblance to cereal evoked mass manufactured processed foods.

Every time I think of laksa, I think of the precarious nature of its existence, the series of coincidences, the specific chaos that when so slightly disturbed would nullify the fact of its creation. But there is a sense of destiny, of inevitability as soon as the story is told. Even as it slips out of our reach, the past is confirmed. And so, it could not have been any other way.

We talked in a sputtering manner, never exchanging more than five sentences between us at a time. Conversing with strangers is hard. At least, it has always been for me. As we talked, I confronted the fact that I was a phenomenally bad conversationalist, and hoped that I would never forget what chicken rice is. Things went by breezily, quickly, and before I knew it, the event had come to an end.

We ended the evening by shaking hands. She told me her name then, as though it had taken us more than an hour to finally come to introductions. The organisers made some final comments. Everyone else was packing up and getting ready to leave as though it was a classroom just before the bell. See you around, she said. I wanted to say more, to hold onto the moment more, or perhaps to have more to hold onto, not because there was anything particularly special about our interactions, but more because, somehow, I could feel time passing, feel the instant getting out of reach. Mm-hmm, was all I mustered as her friend came to get her. I glanced at them as they made their way out of the venue. I waited for the crowd to clear a little as I contemplated the indecipherable series of choices, the precise chaos that had brought together two strangers transiently, like destiny, as though it was always supposed to happen, yet randomly, like the collision of particles.

As the thought passed and the crowd thinned, I shuffled to the exit with the remnants. Emerging from The Substation, I felt unexpectedly disoriented. I took a deep breath, in search of an anchor, and I thought I smelled rain. The sky had, of course, turned dark, and the streets were bathed in the familiar orange glow of Singapore streetlamps. It's the city, I thought, as though I had to be reassured of the fact. It was plain, a familiar character, but it wasn't the same place, charged with bristling strangeness. The city was a facsimile of the city, and in my head, I heard an echo of Eliot: "And what is actual is actual only for one time/And only for one place. It was as though in the intermission of dinner, the city had come to a fork in the road, and through some unseen choice, and that choice alone, its course had changed."[2]

From that divergence, a second city had emerged, one that was ever so slightly incongruent with my internal pulse, just slightly out of sync, a copy invisibly skewed from my experience. The city was no longer the one that I knew, the one that belonged to me. But by the same measure, within the same shimmer of light, I was also no longer the same person, a husk of the memory that I had been cast out of. I had left something behind, or perhaps had been left behind. An echo of Herbert in my mind, who wrote: I live in several times, nonexistent, painfully motionless and painfully in motion and I truly don't know what is given to me and what is taken away forever.[3]

I laughed as I thought of the event and how it was indeed the last meal. The city was gone, and so was the me that had left me behind. I thought of the play of chance, of the impossibility of knowing another, of brief encounters in even briefer lives. I tried to write about it later, when none of it would be true anymore. But even standing there then, I knew that I was narrating it, and I continue to today, this moment, turning it into a tale, weaving, spinning, loom. Every story has a controlling effect on the reality it produces. Every story is a process of violence. We are storytellers, mythmakers, even as these acts destroy what we have, return to us illusions, mislead us, lie to us. But it is the only way to trace the shape of the billowing dark matter of one's corner of the universe.

There's no chance that we will meet again, but sometimes I wonder what I would say, or how we would greet each other. The same greetings that I had so cynically thought of as unnecessary courtesy or facetious pretense, perhaps. Have you eaten? 吃飽了嗎? We ask in spite of the possibility of true answers. Would you like to grab a coffee? Or lunch? A normal meal this time. Another terrible curry. Maybe even McDonald's.

If the evening lingers in us, it also establishes possibility, forms the city, completes time. The city, the self, the moment, multiplying, cascading, and through it, we find the glimmer of joy and the promise of death, the full tang of regret, as we abandon our simulacra, our clones, our reckless stories, our pretensions of omniscience so that conversations may begin.

■ Triptych

2014

I. Permission

I am at the airport, travelling to Europe, when I am stopped by the immigration officer who reviews my passport. He stares at the passport incredulously, and then he says: Are you sure this is you? I want to tell him: What do you mean? Of course it is. But I don't. I just nod sheepishly. I feel embarrassed, or perhaps humiliated, even if I don't understand why. I feel as if I had been found out. Perhaps he too knows that passports are nothing more than a convenient fiction. He looks at me not so much in suspicion but more in comic disbelief, as though I've just played a practical joke that has failed to come off. You're really sure? He asks. I'm not any longer, no, but with my trip to Europe at stake, I just give him my most earnest expression and say yes. What is it that he suspects? Is it my name? Is it my face? Or is it my Singaporean-ness? I can't tell. In the instant, I am no one. Instead, I am a name, a few numbers and a photo. I am a number of stamps and several blank pages. I am my passport: a collection of personal details, a travel history and a potential detainment. It's all I'm left with, and thus I realise that as he holds onto to my documentation, as he doubts my identity, he wields an unnatural, severe power over my momentary existence. He relents eventually and lets me through, pushing the passport back to me across the counter. I receive it gratefully, as though accepting a red packet.

There is no trust at the airport. I suppose it's unfair to say so since the stakes are so high, but I always get the strange twist in my gut whenever I am leaving or entering a country. This shouldn't be surprising as I am a notoriously nervous person, but it is curiously similar to the feeling that I get when I leave a store or a library and am worried about hearing the alarm go off. I've never got into any trouble, no, but the incidents are always embarrassing to me – humiliating, even. Oh, look what you've done. The airport is a friendly, welcoming place, and yet the threat of humiliation always looms over me as I cross the border.

Do you know that Kafka story about the watchman?

> I ran past the first watchman. Then I was horrified, ran back again and said to the watchman: "I ran through here while you were looking the other way." The watchman gazed ahead of him and said nothing. "I suppose I really oughtn't to have done it," I said. The watchman still said nothing. "Does your silence indicate permission to pass?"[1]

Mysterious and terse, this story has troubled me for years. Today the story comes back to me as I think about travel. Permissions, after all, give shape to travel. Each time before leaving the country, I have to log onto the SAF's web portal to notify the Army that I'll be abroad. My passport expires every five years and I have to ensure that it complies with all associated regulations. Each time I leave the country, I nervously check and double-check that I haven't left anything illegal in the luggage. Let me through, I think, as I hand my passport over to the immigration officer. Let me through, I want to tell the customs officer. Let me through, I proclaim once more across the ocean. In a perhaps perverse way, these processes are satisfying to me. They represent travel to me, and more generally, also places.

Today I think that that might be the point of this story, that we cannot resist the idea of permissions. This should not be so surprising since this offers us the possibility of authentication and vindication, as well as the potential for transgression. Without it, freedom, and total freedom, simply throws us into despair. So we build our world on this conceit, permissions upon permissions. We give nations geographical shape by guarding our borders. In a place such as Singapore, where prohibitions and regulations abound, it is also easy to see that we define interior societies with the force of law. Permissions are not the limits to my world but the shape of it.

I'm on my way back from Europe. It's been a long trip and a long flight and I'm exhausted. I step up to the turnstile and the screen invites me to have my passport scanned. Then the gate parts and I am invited to provide my thumbprint as identification. My mother always has problems with these machines. They won't accept her thumbprint. In a way, it is possible to say that her biology denies my mother her citizenship. She used to get worked up at these things, but these days offers little more than sighs of resignation. These gates are baffling. Get used to it.

The machine greets me. I press my thumb down on the scanner. Please wait. Oh no, something's wrong. I look up at the immigration officers, afraid that I've come all this way only to be foiled at my own airport. The screen gives me instructions. Please push your thumb down harder. Something like that. I feel a little stupid. I've come back from the trip with new stories to tell, new things to share, and here I am waiting for a machine to authenticate my identity. I once heard a story about a professor who knew his students by their IC numbers. Here I am being judged by a booklet and a thumbprint.

It lets me pass eventually. Permission granted. I try to keep the self-satisfied smirk on my face to myself. You never know what Immigration might think of it. But I'm looking at my passport, at the photograph; I can't help myself. I'm back home and yet I cannot shake the feeling that I am in fact elsewhere.

II. Echoes

Sometimes I think about Singapore and I think: So many people trying to get in, so many people trying to get out. No one stops. We keep moving, keep travelling, as if in search of the spaces once inhabited by others. Yet we too leave voids behind with each journey. We too leave echoes. And each country, every place, is little more than an assemblage of echoes, signalling from the past and from the future.

The last time that we are on good terms, X picks me up in a cab at a bus stop. It's December 2013 and I'm feeling good about our relationship. We've had ups and downs, to borrow a familiar expression, but the dust seems to have settled, and the imminent turn of the year suggests to me new beginnings. She's not from these parts, but for the time being, she calls the island home – except when she doesn't. She's flying home this afternoon. She gives her mother a call while we're on the expressway. She's speaking in a dialect that I cannot understand. I look out of the window and watch as the outside world passes by silenced. I think about holding her hand. I don't.

When we arrive, she realises that she's running a bit late and I'm left to watch over her luggage as she checks in. I've been quite ill for a couple of days now, and I have to work hard not to fall asleep over it. I'm seated next to a weighing machine and I watch as people fret over suitcases. One or two also worry about their body-mass indices. For a brief moment, I wonder how much luggage makes it in and out of Singapore each day. Then she comes back and apologises about the time. I was hoping that we would be able to have a meal together before I head off, she says. It's okay, I tell her. Plenty of days ahead of us.

She returns shortly after New Year's Day, and then the breakup happens as breakups happen, and a goodbye that I believed was temporary reveals itself to me. I don't ask why, although in the days to come I will sometimes think back to the day at the airport, trying to tease out some kind of secret meaning. I will remember most vividly her expression in the departure hall, her arm raised high up into the air as she waved goodbye. I will come to realise that I was wrong when I read happiness in her face, when I imagined then that it was a sign that she too was ready for our future together. The only meaning I will be left with is that something changed that day. It is a facile meaning, that is, one that occupies the surface of things, but it will be all I have. Maybe this is simply the nature of all departures. Nothing ever stays the same. It's January 2014. She returns, but somehow I've been left behind.

I am in the office hearing my colleagues discuss their latest trips abroad. It irritates me, perhaps because, personally, I've never quite been able to muster the same excitement for travel. I find plenty of excitement in Singapore already. Or perhaps it is jealousy. I too want to get out of this country, with its familiar language and familiar people. I too want to be a tourist, a stranger on foreign soil, at once powerless and anonymous. Self-erasure is the prime product of travel, after all. Being on a flight is sometimes terrifying to me. There in that confined space, without the internet, without any mobile network, and no sign of life outside the window, things lose their shape. Back home, down on the ground, I have a well-established identity, genuine or not. I'm Singaporean and proud to be. Up in the air? Sometimes I'm embarrassed about it. And sometimes they say I'm from Hong Kong, China, Korea, Malaysia, anywhere but the sunny island set in the sea. In being many faces, I have no face at all. Anonymous.

Now and then I think back to the incident with the passport and I wonder why I expend so much effort pretending to be a self that isn't me, just so that I can get out of Singapore in order to be no one. I need to get the hell out of here, if only so that I can begin to miss this place. I need to leave to know what home can mean to me. I need change so that I understand my love of stability. But perhaps most of all, I need to become no one in order to deal with being someone. Here, I am so well-defined, so well-understood. Like this country, there is no element of danger to me. I need to leave to become nobody, and as in the lesson of Odysseus, the greatest of all travellers, *Nobody* can be mighty dangerous.

I look around and I find that it's not hard to find things that I am supposed to miss. I get reminders every National Day. I know I live in a stable and prosperous country that I shouldn't take for granted. I know about the struggle that it took to build this nation. I love the food, the people, the language. This is my country and I like it here. And if I choose to leave it momentarily, it is only with the understanding that without this place, I am no one. That is, when I leave it, I become insubstantial and faceless, little more than a sound.

Recently, C told me that she will be returning to Malaysia after spending the last six years or so here in Singapore. I guess I could say that I always knew that this day was coming. Nonetheless, it still manages to get me down. It's not that it spells the end of a friendship, but departures always herald some irremediable change, some irretrievable loss. I mourn for a friendship irreversibly changed, each secret shared, every incident, every story now awash with the tint of yesterday, deeply pressed under the weight of a chapter closed. Every goodbye is irreversible, a permanent scarring of our delicate histories and futures. We will see each other, we will keep talking, we will fight the good fight. But all goodbyes are permanently carved into our lives. Time shifts. One can never return to the same point. You leave and you never come back. Echoes, echoes.

III. Distance

We live in different times. W is two and a half hours removed from my time zone, less elsewhere and more *elsewhen*. We stay in touch, electronic connections providing us with the illusion of simultaneity. The displacement appears to contract, or perhaps it is concealed, and briefly, it can seem as though we are inhabitants of the same world, the same reality. This is, of course, a lie. No one shares the same time. Our moments are individualised, isolated and infinitesimal. They do not overlap.

Now and then, I think that this is true of every one of us. After all, it is only time that separates us. Our planet is segmented by time, each position corresponding to a time of day, always shifting, shifting. No two people can inhabit the same space and time together. Time divides us all. In this sense, all distances are but differences in time, and all travel is time travel. Let me be facetious and say that the world is a map of moments, and in each moment is a world. We inhabit it as immaterial shapes, always moving, always in transit from one time to another, permanently out of sync. Travel is merely a mode in which this displacement is magnified. Perhaps this is why we travel, to remind ourselves of the persistent distance that exists between all of us. Perhaps we travel in search of lost time to seek the moments and spaces once inhabited by others. Or perhaps it is so that in the headlong rush of return, we find it possible to believe that we do not have to be apart.

Between us there is a great distance, and a mutual longing to over-throw it. We exist in our individual series of moments, each pulse is its own clock, each breath a marker along the indices of our lives – they cannot be shared. And even if our hearts beat synchronised, it is only in conspiracy of the lie that we can share the same days and the same nights. Between us there is a persistent separation, and we go in search of elsewhere in order to create the chance of return and the illusion that we may overcome this final distance between us. And thus we pit ourselves against the grotesque turning of the world. If I miss you, I am mourning our mismatched moments. If I see you, I know that it is little more than an electric ghost that travels down cables, down nerves, a projection of the mind. And if I speak to you, it is not my voice, only an echo, and if I touch you, if I hold your hand, reality taunts us with this insurmountable distance between all souls. I imagine the two of us standing in the rain. You look at me with a faint bewilderment. There is a deep silence between us. The tragedy of it all is not the rain but that we do not share it under the same sky. But I refuse to go quietly. Let me go, let me go to you, give me your last permission. For if we cannot share the moments, then at least we can share our departures, neither times nor locations, just points in a complicated tangle of determinants. Each encounter is a gesture towards the next departure, each meeting framed by our next goodbye, our next acute displacement. Each relationship awaits the final parting of ways. So grant me farewell, grant me facelessness. Let us share our goodbyes, and in doing so, overcome the impossible distance. Let us depart and return, in this strange play of push and pull, of lost and found, of comings and goings. Time and again, we leave one another in order to find each other.

■ Gravity

2020

Bras Basah Complex, named after the area in which it is located, sits across from the famous Raffles Hotel, which is said to have been home, however briefly, to several notable writers, including Conrad and Burgess, at points in its illustrious history. It is bounded by Bain Street, Cashin Street, Victoria Street, and North Bridge Road—the brothers Gilbert Angus and Robert Bain, the prominent Cashin family, Queen Victoria, and the north of Presentment Bridge (now Elgin Bridge). At the bottom, there is a four-storey podium of shops and offices. On the fifth floor, one often finds people exercising, walking their dogs, or gossiping about not-present neighbours. And above that, residential flats split between two HDB apartment blocks, containing the most normal lives in the most normal of environments. It is both a shopping centre and a residential estate, public housing right smack in the middle of the city, where real estate is at a premium. There is a shop selling watches here that looks like it must have had been here from the very beginning, and an art gallery that opened this past week. A complex of connected buildings, but also a complex of intersecting paths, of in-between qualities.

Bras Basah is a Malay name—*beras basah*, misspelled—meaning "wet rice". It refers to a time where the area was a lagoon where boats carrying rice would come through. With land reclamation and urban development, there is hardly a trace of wet rice here today— and certainly no lagoon. Bras Basah Complex has a Chinese name: 百勝樓 (*Baisheng Lou*), which literally means Building of a Hundred Victories. It sounds much more dramatic and important in English, and was likely chosen perhaps because of the way it approximates the sound of "Bras Basah" (百勝, *Baisheng*) while carrying an auspicious implication.

Bras Basah Complex is also colloquially known as "書城" (*Shucheng*), which means "city of books". This is a reference to a time when it housed an impressive number of bookstores, which were consolidated from the greater area of 大坡 (*Dapo*) and 小坡 (*Xiaopo*). While the complex is not actually all that old—it was built in 1980—it is connected to a much larger history of Singapore's publishing industry and Chinese diasporic culture. More directly, whether symbolically or materially it embodies entire cultural histories—and personal ones too. It contains ghosts.

Names are curious things. They can become so removed from their point of origin, can be erroneous, can be overwritten, can resist proper rectification. They can imply histories, but also obscure them.

The story goes that when I was very young, my grandfather would bring both me and my sister to Bras Basah. At that age, I was basically a useless biological machine, with no developed sense of purpose. More importantly, I had hardly any reading faculties and certainly nothing in the way of reading preferences. They say that you can positively influence a child's development during pregnancy with Mozart and reading, so I guess my grandfather believed in similar processes of diffusion. When I was tired from all the walking, I supposedly asked him to carry me. I had already grown considerably by that time, and so my grandfather refused. Reluctantly, I said that I would carry myself.

I have no real recollection of this. I have the haziest impressions of these outings, and even then, I wonder if I've imagined them. I am sceptical of these memories. I don't doubt their veracity—that they actually happened—but I wonder if I've remembered these incidents myself. Perhaps these images came from my own sense of what would be reasonable based on the stories I had been told. When this thought first occurred to me, I immediately remembered the scene in *Blade Runner* where Rick Deckard is talking to Rachael, referencing a spider from her supposed childhood, and he says: "Those aren't your memories; they're somebody else's." As I grew older and my reading preferences became more defined, there seemed to be little reason for the family to visit Bras Basah. I was more into Times the Bookshop, and then later, Borders and Kinokuniya. Those were the places that carried the books that I liked. Growing up, I spoke primarily English, and any situation in which I was forced to speak in Chinese would prove calamitous. I carried this yoke all the way into my teenage years. Bras Basah Complex had, by then, turned into a more commercial space. There were a few bookstores; it had become more notable for the shops that sold musical instruments or art supplies.

I already knew of the 書城 (*Shucheng*) name then, even if I couldn't see the books. I believed it. I could only have imagined it, filling in the gaps according to the stories that I had been told or simply what the name evoked, but I could see this mythical city of books in my mind's eye, almost as if I could remember things that I had no right to.

It's strange to think that given how small the island of Singapore is, and how Bras Basah Complex sits right smack in the middle of the city, that I never quite found my way back to it after those early childhood years. Our paths through spaces, distant and foreign, familiar and convenient, is often so exactly defined that they become more linear narratives than spatial interactions. We have no energy, no need, no motivation—no *time*. Between time and space, you get one or the other sometimes. Our reality is the result of multiple choices and coincidences, the wide sea of possibilities funnelled into the stream of our experience, thinner than a thread.

Sometimes, I found it easy enough to convince myself that the mythical shopping destination of my imagination still existed. But each time I passed by, the reality of things would prove much more disappointing. It was crusty and old, and I almost never stepped in. I rarely had any strong motivation to, though perhaps I didn't want to confront the emptiness that awaited me within the space.

Several years after my childhood adventures with my grandfather, I started a job at Bras Basah Complex. The interview took place on a weekday afternoon. I was quite early, but my anxiousness meant that time slipped by me all too quickly. A bag of nerves, I stepped into the building. There was a pronounced uncanniness. There were some features that looked familiar, certain stores, certain structural features, facets of a place that I must have remembered, heard about, imagined, or gleaned subconsciously from media.

Not long after the interview, I learnt that I had secured the position, and would be able to start work very quickly. Feeling as if I hadn't done very well in the interview, the news came as a surprise, and yet, it also felt like a strange sort of homecoming, like there was underneath it all a slender thread of destiny reeling me towards this place that I had effectively forgotten.

I took some time acclimatising to my new job. Different hours, different commute, new habits. Part of this process was getting to know the space. For such a small building, it concealed many surprises within nooks and crannies—shops hidden from plain view, disused spaces, unusually useful facilities, toilets to avoid. There was none of the mythical City of Books that I had learnt of or perhaps imagined, only details, rigid and practical.

During my university years, I found a book that was a gift from a professor to one of her students in one of the used bookstores. The professor taught at the university I attended. In fact, I had taken one of her classes before, so there was an unusual sense of providence. I turned the page and saw a second note. The recipient of the gift had passed it on to another friend for her birthday. Somewhere further down the line it ended up on those shelves. It always fascinated me that there was a clearly traceable path that the book had taken to arrive in that place at the time, for me to discover it, as though it had been guided by some destiny. I sometimes wonder what happened to that book in the second-hand bookstore. Sometimes I also think that

I am much like that book, swept along by rewritings and erasures, barely making so much as a ripple, perceiving destiny in my stories when there's no such thing as destiny.

There are few bookstores left in this old building. I remember Select Books, run by the indefatigable Lena Lim, and her stories about shoplifters. I remember how The Youth Book Co. was trapped in limbo for a considerable length of time after its owner had passed away and none of his children took up the mantle. I would pass by the store from time to time and wonder when its green signboard would light up again. Basheer Graphic Books remains, a favourite haunt in my youth. In a corner of the building, Xinhua Cultural Enterprises houses an immense book collection belonging to Mr Yeo Oi Sang that still intimidates me with its size, breadth, and depth. His collection and his life story mirror the histories hidden beneath the façade of Bras Basah Complex, of the Chinese publishing industry in the region. Now and then you can see him reading the papers outside the store or tending to his plants.

It feels as though I've known these stories all my life, but the truth is that I learnt of many of them only when I started working in the building, and somehow was drawn to retelling them. They would come to me in various ways—collaged from fragments of remembrances and anecdotal accounts, information I came across in the course of my work, stories I would read in the papers or remember from years and years ago—a patchwork of story parts, truths and half-truths curated from a malady of tedium, leaving only the most exciting portions, extruded into some new reality.

I don't remember what our plans were that day. I only remember that they had failed in some way—a meal that was disappointing, or a show that we were late for. No, we went to the art museum. I feel sure that we went to the art museum, even if no impressions of our time there remain. You wanted to go to Bras Basah Complex, you said.

I can see us walking down the rain-swept streets. You lead the way because it's not an area that I frequent. I see myself shuffling along gingerly because my shoes prove too slippery. I'm looking for art supplies, you say. Do you want to come along? We cross the road at the traffic junction, turn around, walk past the library, and then let the rickety escalators take us up to the fourth floor. Barely a word passes between us.

We walk up the stairs and you start to look at the stationery. I merely tag along, silent witness, moral support. I am out of my depth. I have no knowledge of arts and crafts, only the trauma of flailing away during the classes in my schooling years. The sound of footsteps, the squeak of shoes, outside, the glare of the sun. Do you see it? you say. It's not here, you say. I nod, make some sort of noise in agreement. It's just paper, but I barely have any idea what I'm looking at.

Somewhat disappointed in your eventual haul, you pay for the few items you manage to find. Then you say that you have to rush home to help your brother with something. I nod. You say goodbye like it's any other day, but every goodbye here feels final.

To be frank, I've never seen my grandfather reading. I didn't know if he was much of a reader at all. In spite of the childhood memories and his clear belief in the importance of a cultural education, I can't say that he was ever into books—and certainly not literature. The only book I can be certain that he read was one that I had lent to him when he was in the hospital, thinking it would keep him entertained. It was《城門開》or *City Gate, Open Up* by Bei Dao, and after he had completed it, he mentioned repeatedly that some of the terms used were from the Beijing dialect.

Encouraged by the success of this recommendation, I lent him a book by Gao Xingjian. He was in the hospitals a lot by that time, and I wondered if it would kickstart a book-reading renaissance for him. The book was《靈山》*Soul Mountain*, perhaps Gao's most famous work and also a tome of considerable heft. I thought that a long book would keep him occupied for a decent amount of time. Among the greatest enemies in any prolonged hospital experience is boredom.

Some months later, after he had been in and out of different hospitals a few times, I asked if he enjoyed the book, but he couldn't seem to recall that I had lent anything to him. It was lost for several months, vanished without a trace. A theory surfaced that my aunt had been overzealous when tidying up their place for them. At that point, I grew resigned, convinced that the book was lost forever.

I contemplated purchasing a second copy. By that time, I had already started working in Bras Basah Complex, and every so often,

I would look up the book in the few surviving bookstores within. It wasn't difficult to find. In fact, I would always come across the same edition—an anniversary edition published in Taiwan that included photographs—and came close to purchasing it on several occasions. I'm not sure why I looked for the book exclusively in Bras Basah Complex. Perhaps I was encouraged by the memories—experienced or inherited—of my childhood, or perhaps it just seemed to fit the narrative that one goes to Bras Basah to find Chinese books. It was also helped by the fact that there weren't all that many Chinese bookstores in Singapore, with most of them having to prune their inventories to make space for better-selling products.

Or perhaps it was because I intuited that the place held particular significance for my grandfather. One time, he asked me to buy a Chinese dictionary from Bras Basah Complex because he knew that it was where I worked. He explained that, having not done much writing over the years, he could feel the language slipping away from him. The City of Books narrative clearly still held great meaning for him, or maybe he was remembering the times we had spent together when I was much smaller and he was still sprightly. Maybe I was trying to continue his story in a place that I had wilfully believed it should continue.

This indecision over whether I ought to purchase a new copy continued for months until one day, I saw my book at my grandparents' place, stored neatly in a plastic crate. By that time, both my grandfather and aunt had died. My grandmother didn't even know that it was mine. She returned it to me and smiled briefly, glad that she was able to help, and then the smile disappeared again—hardly unusual, as she had always seemed quite distracted in the past few months. She had lost too much too quickly.

presences as thin as whispers. Two people, two shadows, standing in the open plaza. Us, a version of us, but no longer one which we can lay a claim to, now lost or just forbidden. The rectangular frame of the architecture above us, unfolds into vastness, into void, the night sky taking on the mantle of a god. That night, we passed by this same building, passed through it, assimilated it into some tale.

I described it to you as one describes a tourist attraction, contrary to my intentions. I wanted you to feel at home, wanted to remove the barriers to experience, but perhaps set up more instead. In the end, it should not have been surprising. I was an outsider to this bastion, I did not belong in my memories. The door was shut, leaving a space most unresponsive, most inert, a sullen façade staring at us, unreadable gaze.

the city surrounds. District, distance. Disjunct, disconnect. Together we stepped through the plaza, looked at the pathways, listened for the sounds that weren't there, ghost-voices, wave patterns. Together, seekers of endings.

quiet, dull above you who are missing, comforting, unnerving. It was awful, yet paradoxically calming, and we, survivors of a deathly stillness, poets of an unnamed eschatology. It wasn't the last evening we spent together—and yet it may as well have been.

I walk through the place with equal measures of pity and disgust. Officially painted murals sit next to scratches and scrawls on the walls. Cockroaches nest in the rubbish chutes. Benches decorated with last night's beer bottles. There is a staircase that perpetually smells of urination. There is another where I once saw teens getting their hands all over one another. The rain washes grime onto concrete, pattern, draught, a chart of the indecipherable relief of time.

The place is *lived in*, unlike so many of the buildings around it, sterilised, maintained, continuously renewed or replaced. In contrast, Bras Basah Complex is bodily, alive, ageing, bearing scuffs and scars, sputum, secretions, various disjecta.

Yet it is also a place that I want to return to, and yet am unable to—nostalgia, the pain of not being able to return. The repulsive body and the pristine memory, the same disconnect that Barthes describes between the voice and the grain of the voice, the same separation between identity and being. Biology and story, machine, memory.

Today, I went into the complex to see that renovation works were underway. Lift upgrading works, a fresh coat of paint. Stores closing, opening, moving, renewing themselves. Losses, replacements. Piecemeal changes, shedding skin. But like in the quandary of the Ship of Theseus, how does a place remain a place? Why do we imagine such stability for our places?

Places are not vessels for memories, but they can give such an impression when so many lines converge. I keep wandering the area,

I keep walking down the same paths, the shops that are different and yet the same. I watch as scenes transform or vanish, as things are effaced and disappeared. My memories of those outings with my grandfather have also been obscured, transformed into memorable anecdotes. Is the unfortunate effect of writing to turn even the most mundane of stories into unnecessarily attractive narratives?

The City of Books no longer exists, and perhaps it never did—at least not physically. What is there is a body, ageing, decaying, excreting, but also a body of changes, the traces of which are often erased or invisible, but in the tangle of old and new, in the tensions between that which departs and that which remains, a picture emerges of absences, glorious histories, delicate stories. The thread hints at an imperceptible web. The memories bubble to the surface, lost friendships, stolen glances, regrets, moments too mundane to be turned into stories. Then I see my grandfather, in tinted glasses and clothes unfamiliar to me, an impression pieced together using the identikit of photographs

and myself, young again, small again, only just starting to recognise words, only just beginning to discover the mechanisms of gravity.

SOLARIS
2015

sadness comes back and comes back
as fragrant and lush as the grass

Yu Xuanji

Giuseppe Arcimboldo, *Spring*. 1563.

ONE ■ INTERLOPER

I

One day a few years ago, I agreed to meet a friend at the Law Faculty campus of the National University of Singapore. The campus sits on the edge of the Botanic Gardens. Having arrived a little earlier than we agreed, I took a short stroll through the Gardens, taking care not to stray too far from the campus. I made my way back, punctual, but my friend was nowhere to be seen. I waited for her calmly, but I began to get nervous after fifteen minutes. I couldn't be certain if something had cropped up, if something had happened to her, or if I had simply been mistaken about the time. I texted her to no avail. I thought about calling, but it was the examination season and it seemed likely that I would be disturbing her revision. So I simply waited in the ambiguous border between the campus and the Gardens. I was embarrassed that I had quite possibly been forgotten by my own friend. I began pacing around, pretending to take a walk in the garden, checking my phone constantly even though it wasn't buzzing. I gazed up at the trees, kicked pebbles, watched sparrows hop. It was all busywork, intended to create the impression that there was a lot going on. I wonder if I felt guilty that nothing was actually happening. Or perhaps it was to avoid having to confront the embarrassment of having been abandoned. There, around me, was the garden, quiet and peaceful, concealing the constant breathing and a constant decay. In contrast, I was fidgeting and gesturing, trying to hide that I really had nothing to do. In this perverse performance, I attempted to look natural in front of invisible eyes. Ironically, I was probably the most unnatural thing in the garden.

My distress was difficult to explain. Perhaps it was because being forgotten by your friends is inherently embarrassing, but also philosophically disturbing. Not that anyone could tell by looking at me. Yet, why else would I be alone, waiting in the midday sun? The quietness of the Gardens didn't help, and my being neither here nor there was mirrored by the space, the ambiguous border between the city and the garden. Gardens are sites of tension, positioned between the natural and the manmade. The word garden derives from the Old Germanic and implies enclosure, and as most people know, every enclosure has two sides: It is an isolated space that imprisons, but by the same measure, it protects its internal space from an invading exterior reality. Such an idea lends itself well to the garden, but this dialectical conception can come across as being a little too straight-forward. After all, aren't gardens a form of curated nature, or even unnatural nature? Conceptually, they are a grotesque conjunction of organic material and human interference.

Nature lends itself to curation in the first place. Plants bend themselves towards the sunlight. Tree roots snaking around obstacles. Branches adjusting to pressure. Words and pictures carved into tree trunks, like marks, like scars, bodily traces. Knots, stumps. Each contortion or diversion is a mark of time, a message, a negotiation, or an interruption. This biological behaviour is exploited in a systematic fashion in many gardens, which are in concept the organisation of the organic into carefully defined spaces. In the most basic sense, the garden is an archive, within which is contained the collective memory of the living and the dead. In many cases this is a hidden memory, but memory nonetheless, remembrances of former things, and remembrances of things that are to come with those that shall come after. The garden remembers, just as we remember, and in rare cases, these remembrances overlap.

Every now and then, I think of that moment in the Gardens, and details return to me in trickles. I think I recall, for example, what I was wearing that day. I recall also the face of a passing dog, though I couldn't for the life of me tell you what the owner looked like. I remember the occasional call of birds. The colours of leaves. A caterpillar. These remembrances sprout from that one starting point, in directions that I seem to have little influence over. Thus memory unfurls, disordered, illogical—even free. Free of designated purpose, free of importance, free until I fold it into my story.

I waited, stupidly, for almost three hours that afternoon. I remember noticing how the sun had changed its position by the time my friend showed up. After a brief and disappointing meal with her, I decided that I would spend more time in the Gardens, as if to make up for the effort of having made the journey. I made my way gradually, sweating, to the Sundial Garden. Its stillness and silence unnerved me. There was no one there and nothing stirred. Unsure of what to do, I was drawn to the sundial that stood quietly, solemnly in the middle of the garden. The sunlight was weak. I watched as time passed.

The most unmistakeable quality of the sundial garden is its honesty. Its pronounced aesthetic announces its condition as construction. There is no confusion that it was carefully designed and manually installed. I am told that the Botanic Gardens evolved according to a style known broadly as the English landscape garden, which is a departure from the formal approach to gardens—notably the French formal garden style—dominant before the middle of the eighteenth century. This explains the stark contrast between the Botanic Gardens as a whole and the small sundial garden housed within it. The latter is far more formal in character, clearly favouring symmetry and simple shapes preferred by the human mind. It is an imposition of order, perhaps, using familiar shapes and recognisable symbols, signs relating to human discourse. The sundial—simple geometry

tracing basic shapes with the position of the sun—is pure signification describing the passing of time and our place in the solar system.
This piece of human ingenuity stands in a curated version of the natural world, quietly marking time.

This curious conjunction of material stone and immaterial
shadow was invented to measure our relationship to the sun and
stars, an index of time and memory. Thus, it demonstrates our inex-
tricability from the natural forces. Everyone casts a shadow under
the sun, and this shadow indicates the time of day, our position in
the context of the solar system. The sundial's time reflects our own
shadow-time, running separately from the time on our clocks and
computers. In fact, every so often a second is added to compensate
for the slowing pulse of the planet. These are called leap seconds,
and they are vital in maintaining synchronicity between the caesium clock standard of time—a rhythm of atoms—and the length of
days—the rhythm of the planets. The addition of each new second is
veritably invisible, a quiet adjustment to the index of civilisation, like
individual grains added to a mound of sand. This time is a meticu-
lously preserved human endeavour, a carefully maintained index of
our civilisation. Sometimes I wonder if we could simply let it go, forget it, allow the caesium clock to outpace the sun. What's the worst
that could happen? The universe would churn on, indifferent to our
concepts and indices. Only a matter of record, so to speak, and yet...
This might be why it is so important to keep these times in sync. It
is a matter of archiving, a system of reference with which we access
human history. In this way, time is the greatest of human inventions.

It is the way in which we talk about our memory and existence, and the way we align ourselves with the stars. It gives a name to each moment in our collective history. It provides a system of reference points, of years and days and hours, down to the minute, down to the second, where each subjective moment can be remembered, indexed, and defined relative to another. Time—our ticking clocks and digital numbers, our records and calendars—is at the heart of all our stories, our histories given form by the light and the darkness. Like the garden, time is an archival project—arguably the largest of them all—revealing our addiction to or perhaps more disturbingly our dependence on organisation.

Now and then I return to the same spot to see the ghost of me, standing on the borders of places, the boundaries of things, nervously waiting for my friend. Perhaps I was nervous because I felt exposed as a human sham, separated, naked in the garden, ashamed as in the biblical myth, lost in memory but a slave to time. The garden reveals that it is not nature or memory but the human that is enclosed, our minds so entrenched in our logics and systems that we have trapped ourselves, made ourselves outsiders in the world at large. Gardens are an archival approach to nature, much as the index of time engages with memory. Yet one finds in the garden's many contradictions a path. It grows and breathes, but somehow it stays the same. It is also an archived nature, a reordered nature, a human-nature. The garden is a place of memories but also a place of the now, where two seemingly incompatible pieces can seem to coexist, where human logic negotiates with natural force. It is a place of im/possibility. Here there is a way out. Here I need wait no longer. Thus I watch my ghost pass into shadow, exorcised, now an echo, now a sigh. Going, going, gone.

The sundial garden was installed in 1929 by Eric Holttum, director of the Botanic Gardens at the time. The centrepiece of the garden, a small sundial atop a square pillar, was designed by his wife Ursula, and is one of the few remaining original features of the plan. The garden's lily ponds and Grecian statues were added much later, and I tend to imagine that the original garden looked very different from the way it does now. If nothing else, the garden has preserved its shape, a distinctly rigid rectangular space. Standing in contrast to the more naturalistic or organic tone of the rest of the Botanic Gardens. This contrast, perhaps, is its greatest feature. The statues in particular are a peculiar sight, a little old-fashioned, evoking a time far in the past, yet perhaps not far enough. Once I had come here to take wedding photos for a friend, and the couple very quickly began parodying, the statues, as though it came quite naturally to them to mimic them and poke fun of them.

The sundial garden is very well-defined. Here the paths, short as they may be, exert a curious power upon the landscape. They are boundaries, defining the limits of the garden and drawing interior shapes. They are also imprints, human marks on an otherwise naturalistic landscape, reflections of the mind of their designer or perhaps just a simple I-was-there, like an enduring footprint.

Outside of the small rectangular border of the sundial garden, most of the paths in the Botanic Gardens have an arguably more natural quality to them, gentler, less angular, weaving their way around trees and stone as though responding to the terrain. Nevertheless, in spite of their differences, all of the Gardens' paths are its constitution. Let's start with its shapes and lines. Naturalistic or not, formal or not, the paths delineate the shape of the garden, the boundaries of it, the routes within, and all of its interior possibilities.

The paths reveal the garden's overlapping forms. For example, there is the physical garden, the embodied multitudes within its boundaries, living, growing, decomposing, cycles upon cycles. There is also the symbolic garden, described with a map, much like a word or a graphic. There is also the garden of the mind. Over time, I've developed a reliable mental map of the Botanic Gardens. Nevertheless, my sense of navigation is far from exceptional and I am always one wrong turn away from being grossly late for appointments. As a result, I often make slightly absurd concessions when meeting friends or attending weddings, arriving twenty minutes, even half an hour before it's time—I arrive far ahead of time in order to arrive just in time.

Another idea of the garden that I am interested in is arguably harder to pin down. Each of these paths has a destination, a fixed trajectory, a finite length. As we begin to walk down any one of them— even before we do so—we understand that each path is known and that there is a type of foreknowledge associated with it. It is a form of predestination—the path leads us to where we end up. It is also the confidence that someone has gone ahead, that our route has already been mapped. It is in other words a promise that all roads lead somewhere. Having been defined, paths allow for deviations and possibilities. To explore these is to actively engage with the paths—and the garden—to recognise the transience of experience and the promising uncertainty of the moment. One might even call it a performance. This is the garden as shaped by experience and configured by the mind, a garden of possibilities.

Having secured a writing residency, I was to commence a project focusing on the Singapore Botanic Gardens, but the prospect of it was unnerving. Yet, every piece of writing is undertaken with great uncertainty—without knowing where you will go, or where you will end up—and it is only in this condition that we write. Every essay, every sentence, every word must maintain the possibility of not-knowing, up until the end. This is the energy that drives writing's basic action. But there was, and still is, something different about this proposition, perhaps not just unnerving, but also daunting. Where do I begin? With what material do I work? Most of all, why does the garden make me feel the way that it does? There is so little available to me and so much that is baffling.

Keen to assuage my anxieties, I went to the Gardens one afternoon under the pretence of taking a walk when I was really interested in getting a feel for what I was getting into ahead of the project. I had intended to spend the day doing research and taking photographs, less with a specific objective in mind and more to get in the mood for writing. Unfortunately, the stifling weather would soon prove to be my undoing. The dense vegetation in the area of the Botanic Gardens seemed only to drive the humidity in the air up. Writing was the very last thing on my mind. Frankly, I can't quite explain the psychology at work here. Faced with the uncooperative weather, any sensible person would simply walk away. But no, I had already come this far, and I wasn't going to make my way back home without a fight. Thus, I stepped through the Bukit Timah gate and into the Gardens proper, and from that point onwards, there was no turning back.

With my mind clouded by the heat-haze, I walked aimlessly, guided purely by the paths available to me and the turns that struck my fancy. I noticed that every other visitor seemed exceptionally composed and collected, while there I was in a sweat, trying to catch the breeze—which, unfortunately, was warm at best. None of it was of any use, of course, as I made my way into the Gardens with my shirt soaked and my mind all over the place. Eventually, I decided that it was not enough simply to walk through a small section of the Gardens and calling it a day. I reasoned that even if I didn't get any work done, I had to feel and seem as though I was getting things done—the sensation and the impression of effort, if you will, a personal obligation as well as a matter of public image. After all, I didn't want to seem like the fool or coward who had come to the place only to be turned away by the weather. So I resolved to go from one end of the Gardens to the other, believing that it would be enough of a struggle to justify my long bus ride in the morning. I would also have to appear to be hard at work at something. While the garden is a place of leisure and no one would fault you for drifting through it without a sense of purpose, this didn't sit well with the fact that no one could possibly be out purely for a walk under this weather. There had to be a good and proper reason for my exertions. I simply couldn't bear the thought that I would return emptyhanded.

I decided that I would take photographs along the way to demonstrate to others—and myself—that I wasn't at the Gardens just for fun. There was no mistaking a photographer at work, after all. Thus, I went about my way, disguising my discomfort and dishevelled demeanour. I wore a stern expression, as if to say that I should be taken seriously. The truth was, the weather was draining, and I hardly had any inclination to do any proper work. I went through the motions, snapping away as I imagined that I was supposed to, producing pictures that I would, for the most part, delete later in the day. I had no objectives in mind, no checklist to cross off, simply a direction and the time of day—not too much time, but not too little. Armed with little more than a handkerchief against the weather, however, I was rapidly turning into a sweating sack of a person. I persisted. I wasn't working as much as I was posing, performing, creating the illusion of a man who was to be taken seriously.

In reality, I was little more than an undignified caricature. How did I end up once again in a ridiculous situation where I felt obliged to pretend that I was doing what I was not? Why did I feel the compulsion to stage an entirely unnecessary and completely silly performance? Why did I feel some sense of responsibility, some force of obligation? Indeed, why did I feel obliged about anything at all? I realised that I was driven by a sense of unease, a feeling that I didn't fit in. I was a disruptive presence in an image of the garden that did not include me. I felt as if I didn't belong, like some kind of bad undercover agent. In other words, the wholeness of the garden— nature, visitors, staff—was perfect and at odds with my intrusion.

One might argue that any action undertaken with the awareness of being watched is a performance. That said, I think we can all agree that my woes had blossomed out of rather ridiculous logic and I was very much a fool making a mountain out of a molehill. Nevertheless, while at some level this was a simple public place, I felt as if I could not blend in, and was suffering for it. In this combination of circumstances and psychology, I felt that I had to justify my presence in the place. Is there such a thing as proper etiquette in the garden? Of course there had to be, I told myself, so perhaps the question really was: Is the garden different from other public places, and if so, how?

The garden is an alien space, one that stands apart from our daily life. This is particularly true in Singapore, where the domestic garden is something of a rarity. Even though the country has been termed the Garden City, it is more a city infiltrated by the greenery of a garden than a garden itself. The garden is an atypical space which stands apart from the more urban areas. The ways in which it does so are numerous and not so easily described, but it engenders a feeling of otherness. Foucault described the heterotopia, a place that is both of the mind and of the corporeal, a place that is both and is neither. The garden is, after all, a curious overlapping of opposites and extremes, city and nature, manmade and organic, physical and imaginary. It seems only fitting that I would feel like an outsider inside of the place, apart from the proceedings, from nature, institution, and visitor alike. Which is to say, amid all of this beauty, in the middle of some mysterious organic order, I was not at ease. Not only did I perform for invisible eyes, I had also become extremely self-conscious of my performance.

All public life is in fact the staging of this battle. To preserve one's individuality and to avoid the disturbing fate of facelessness, one tries to stand out from the crowd. However, one must also avoid standing out too much to avoid becoming a target. I must conform, but not at the expense of my total self, or rather, not at the cost of totalising myself. I must not blend in too perfectly. This explains a great many things in day-to-day life, including how fashion works. However, there within the Botanic Gardens, the balance was scaled differently. I was desperate to blend in and completely unable to. Hence the performance that one might argue was only ever in my head.

We can think of performance naïvely as any act that under-scores the passing moment. Every act or action itself is a statement of the irretrievability of time, but performance is a way of thinking and acting that focuses on this condition. Performance occurs in time, and invites a reading with that understanding. In this sense, the experience of the garden is a performance. And even apart from my frivolity and awkwardness, we must accept that the garden is only what we make it out to be. It is the crossing of paths and the spotting of animals. It is the walk, the conversation, the meeting of the eyes. It is the path that we trace, the geometries that we form with our feet, in our minds. My walk is my performance, through which I conceive of the garden, make it anew, affirm its existence and reimagine it time and again, like the turning of seasons or the cycles borne by both the living and the dead.

I proceed from myself. I can only proceed from myself. It is where I have to begin. I know that I find the garden beautiful, but also that it makes me uncomfortable. Inscribed around the sundial are the words "what thou seekest is a shadow", and perhaps this best describes my task. I am seeking something that is but isn't. I must first accept the garden's heterotopic nature, its state of being in between two extremes or opposites, the seemingly impossible state of being. Only then can I find what it is that the Gardens mean to me. So my writing becomes my performance, and through this lens, by foregrounding the passing of time and the transience of being, I proceed. I walk down the paths in search of understanding, of memory, of love. In walking, I enact the Gardens. And hence it comes to life.

II

There are certain things that I remember only in name. I know, for example, that as a child, I visited a number of different Malaysian states. I was in Penang once. The only thing I remember about it is that it was my first time on a plane, but disappointingly, I cannot actually remember my first time on a plane. Instead, all I have is a photograph of me and my sister sitting side by side in our economy class seats. That is, I'm certain that it happened, even though I do not have any substantial memory of the event. I also remember that we travelled with my aunt to Kuala Lumpur. We took the train there back when the old railway station at Tanjong Pagar was still active. But I can't recall anything about the train except that it shook and wobbled like we were in Indiana Jones's *Last Crusade*—although this certainly is no great feat of recollection, for most trains of the sort wobble and shake in the same manner. I remember thinking upon arrival that I was in a dangerous place because it was all so new to me, but beyond the large grey rectangle that was the face of the hotel, no images come to mind. The last fact I retain from my time in the Malaysian capital is that I was too afraid to enter the Batu Caves, despite being unable to summon any memory of being there. There was also a beach trip with the family in Malaysia. I don't remember travelling there, but I do remember having my head in the water and finding it hard to breathe. That was the first time that I thought I was on the edge of drowning, the first time I thought I was going to die. I also remember a family friend catching a small translucent jellyfish in a plastic bag. I think the plastic bag was small, two by three inches, perhaps, and the jellyfish was devoid of any detail. I remember the creature fondly.

I remember the event, but nothing in detail. The remembrance of things past comprises vague impressions of places and faint sketches of people. What I can recall tend to be the occurrences, not images or sounds, not smells, not sensations, but that something happened. I can describe events. I can narrate them. It is not difficult to verify them with accounts and testimonies. However, this authentication of our shared reality confirms two things: that there are slippages that exist in our attempts to remember, and that there is no direct access to our memories. There is always the need to fill in the details and to narrate things such that they make sense. Memory is substantiated or even accessed via fabrication. Or maybe we should say that memory is composition. Julio Cortázar described it as the language of feeling, "a dictionary of faces and days and smells which repeat themselves like the verbs and adjectives in a speech, sneaking in behind the thing itself, into the pure present, making us sad or teaching us vicariously"[1]. Memory is a language that requires composition and construction.

This is a dangerous game to play with memory. To realise that it is not details, just the stories, just the thoughts and the names, that one remembers, one swiftly becomes drawn to the possibility that almost nothing real is retainable. Over time, I've come to realise that even what vague impressions I have in my mind cannot be trusted. At some level, these are merely images and sounds that I've constructed, impressions that I have fabricated from a combination of remembrance and reimagining. Is perception not after all illusion?

It is a description appropriate for all of history, but when the history is one's own, an existential tension is attached to it, for if we do not remember our pasts ourselves, who else can we count on to do so? And so it is possible to accept or even to be confronted by the fact that there is no infallible authentication, because all recollection is imperfect and all moments are or will be forever lost. But we do not live solely in the now, if anything we live in our memories, and so we remind ourselves to act, to tell our stories, write our words, leave our traces across a tenuous psychic landscape, to resist the possibility that there was nothing there, a constant reaffirmation of one's existence. Nothing inhabits our past and nothingness haunts it, and thus we spin our own tales, over and over, eager to recuperate the irrecoverable, and thus we become our images, and thus we become ghosts.

I can't speak for everyone, but this method seems to be the basis of my memory, and as such, it also characterises what I can remember of the Gardens. These memories are generally hazy, indefinite, and irrecoverable. Like detectives, we piece together the past from clues, with logic, following some recognisable sequence, via imagination. There is often nothing certain about the past. It is always a fabrication—it has to be—because it is necessary that at some level, we deny that it is always slipping away.

One day, however, when presented with a photograph, I was compelled to remember. It was a photograph of me at a young age standing under some flowers that I was told was taken at the Botanic Gardens. The colours in the photograph had developed and continue to develop a copper tone, reducing the detail and contrast in the picture, as if to remind me that in the fullness of time, all things are equalised. This photograph embodied to me my first hurdle in writing about the Gardens, because I remembered nothing about it. Having so little to go upon, I could only imagine what it was like to be in those shoes, under that sun, and within that frame of mind. None of my efforts were really effective or very meaningful, of course, but when you see a picture of yourself from far in the past, you naturally do your best to see if you can recall anything from the time.

The photograph in question was part of a moderately large collection, which my mother brought out from the cupboard when she learnt that I was embarking on this project. She told me of these photographs of me as a child, almost an infant, at the Botanic Gardens, and unearthed them from the sizeable collection of childhood photographs featuring me and my sister. As the years went by, I would appear in fewer and fewer photographs, perhaps too self-conscious to feel comfortable about them. As such, this collection is still the most comprehensive visual archive of any extended period of my life.

There were fewer photographs of me in the Botanic Gardens than she had believed. (There were, however, several of my sister and the family.) My mother elaborated to say that the family would go down to the Gardens quite often, back when my father still had a car. (I remember less the look and make of the family cars and more the texture of the seats, the smell of air fresheners, and the sights outside the window, and more just the idea of family outings.) Back then, there really wasn't much in the way of recreation where we were living, and in our family's leisure time, they would usually drive us out of the neighbourhood in search of what seemed like attractively middle-class activities to them. By the time I was born, however, they had perhaps grown tired of the drive down to the Gardens, and in a few years, a variety of conveniences would sprout within our neighbourhood, rendering it much easier for us to distract ourselves. Our corner of the island had become less of a jungle and blossomed as a neighbourhood. In a way, the improvements to public transport and roads made it easier for us to visit the Gardens, but in another, the Gardens had seemed so much further than before. There seemed to be no reason to abandon convenient entertainment for a day out in the Gardens. In fact, the frequency of the family's visits to the

Gardens had declined so greatly I probably visited the place as a child under a dozen times.

I looked at the photographs, trying to return to that time and that place. I tried to remember, to return, but my efforts were in vain. I still don't remember what occurred on that day in that place. Have I forgotten? Perhaps I never truly remembered? Deep down, I knew the endeavour was futile, but I did not want to lose a part of my own history out of a want of trying. I wasn't so interested in the hard facts, not data but perspective. Could I in other words see the world as a child again? It was impossible to return to the garden of my childhood, but at least I needed to know if there was anything left in my memory that I could conjure, even if it was just a feeling, an emotion, or the faintest of sensations.

This is, of course, something of a thematic cliché as far as gardens are concerned. The desire to return to the garden has certain biblical echoes. I was trying to return to a period of innocence, to a time before words, for it was precisely the shortage of words that motivated the Edenic act of naming. I was in search of a type of paradise, and in recognising this, I knew also that I was basically in search of the impossible. The myth of Eden is defined by its impossibility, delineated by the notion that things have already slipped away, that things *will always already have slipped away.* Paradise deathless and pure cannot retain its shape. For humans in our postlapsarian condition, an idea or a space cannot exist until it is vulnerable to change. Something must happen, something must change, in order to give a place definition.

In lieu of recollection, I began to make up stories. For instance, I assumed that the Gardens had not changed too much beyond what I knew of it, and that the sights, sounds, and smells had the consistency of more recent days. I imagined myself in my shoes, too large for my infant feet, clumsily lumbering around and pretending that I was walking. I conceived of myself as the embarrassment that we all are at that tender age. I saw my mother in the fashion of yesterday, and my father when he still had his hair. His smile was still the same smile, the one I carelessly emulate today. Was my sister there? I didn't know, but I suspected that she had to be. In this way, an impression of the time was formed. This is the way memory works, then, the connection of points like the joining of dots. It *must* have happened in such and such a way, and so it did. Narrative logic, cause and effect, one thing leading to another, a constant process of refashioning. The past becomes a patchwork woven together by one's ability to compose an attractive and believable story. In this way, the imagination becomes both the paths and the boundaries, guiding the ways in which I remember and in which I make myself again.

One remembers through a constant process of making narratives and even fictions. Memory is a process of improvisation, and even a performance. And so I begin to fill in these memories, to add lines and colours, to explain each occurrence with a combination of reasonable guessing and logic, for much like composing a story or writing an essay, there are things in memories which cannot be avoided—some things have to be established, some things have to be explained, sentences inescapable, paragraphs unavoidable, pulled together by some logical gravity. In some ways, we would want to remember in the way a computer remembers, retrieving perfect data from magnetic disks, the information infallible, unambiguous, complete, and stable for the foreseeable future. Human memory, however, is porous, unreliable, vastly incomplete, and without clear delineations of the true and the false. If we are to understand the garden as a heterotopic or in-between place, then we must also understand memory as its own heterotopia. In the practice of memory, the shape of the dialectic, underpinned by two extremes or opposites, becomes blurred, out of focus, allowing for overlaps and ambiguities. In memory, as in the garden, it is fruitless to search for clear delineations between categories.

Going into this project, I believed that one of my first hurdles would be to separate truth from storytelling, because otherwise, it seemed that I would only be lying to any readers of this text. Yet, that sense of responsibility was tempered by the understanding that all fiction has roots in the factual, but more importantly that all fact contains a measure of fiction. This, then, became the basis from which I proceeded, because in understanding this entanglement, one also accepts that even if all writing is fabrication, at least all writing is true.

This is a fashioning, the remaking of something lost in order to recover that which is confined to the slippages. If these are images that I am unable to trust, they are also images (from *imago*, also the root of "imagine") that I can do nothing but trust, for they give my past a substance and almost a tangibility that I would much rather be in possession of. The example is extreme, but the point is that we protect our own pasts through our memories. What else could authenticate my childhood? I am, of course, not making the argument that I have no childhood if I cannot remember it, but certainly without a history, the term becomes an empty shell. If there is no meaning, substance, or value attached to said childhood, then it begs the existential crisis. Memory is all I have. I am compelled to remember.

Maybe it is better to see these processes of memory as a form of storytelling. The composition of stories depends on the connection of one point to another. In the same way, I must have filled in these blanks in my memory. In the end, these are just stories and storytelling. There is nothing to suggest that these formulations should not be believed. And if it is difficult to believe that our memories are to some significant degree fabricated, it may be harder still to accept that they do not detract from the truth of the remembrance. In this way, as functions of time that occur immediately, they exceed their obvious relationship to the past. Maybe it would be easier to think of them as projections and extrapolations which sit in the uncomfortable position between truth and fabrication. This implies that at some level, my memories are not trustworthy, but sometimes, all I have are voids and vacuums, and in those cases, there is a force, stronger than mere temptation, to fill in the blank space. The mind cannot resist stories, language, and fabrication.

This, perhaps, is why people write. Writing, both the act and its product, is a seduction, and this aspect of it speaks to both the natural order of things as well as the nature of the self. It is not difficult to understand the desire to fill in blank pages and canvases, partly because our physical reality can sometimes seem averse to emptiness—water rapidly inhabits a container and air is quick to fill a vacuum. But more insidious perhaps is the demiurgic power that is often associated with a creative (pre)occupation, though perhaps less so in these postmodern times. We are addicted to storytelling because we are addicted to creating. A writer creates little beyond arrangements of words, but from these meagre means spring a variety of intangible things—discourses, emotions, worlds. Perhaps the primary power of writing is that in whatever form—poetry, fiction, letters, essays—it has its basis in storytelling. In that respect, both activities echo each other. Perhaps the only form of creation truly available to us is the creation of the self.

In remembering, in telling stories, in writing, truths and tales alike are summoned, put together, composed of our own volition. In a sense, our memories are stories we tell ourselves over and over again, until they can hold their shape or take on substance, until we can make ourselves believe that we are what we know ourselves to be. The fact of the matter is that nothing is stable, especially not memory, which requires a constant re-performance or re-presentation just to preserve its consistency. Thus our lives are chained to stories, to the ways in which we fashion our identities and present ourselves, but also the way that we reveal the substance of existence.

French film theory pioneer Bazin writes: "All the arts are based on the presence of man, only photography derives an advantage from his absence."[2] What is the advantage here? And can I truly be thought to be absent? That, in the photograph, is me, if only because all signs point to it being so. Who else could it be? But I look at the photograph again (it is here at my desk), and I struggle to come to terms with it. That is not me. I is another (Rimbaud)[3], I is someone else, a construction, and sometimes a sham. I go to the garden in search of I. Each footstep, each picnic, each breath; each recollection, each anecdote, each voice testifies to the porosity of memory, to its gaps and its constant slipping-away, but it also allows each remembrance to surface, unveiling the structure of my reality, for the present moment is always already gone, but pieces of the past can be retained or resurrected in the realm of signs and symbols, in the mind, in the memory. And what does it matter if it is fact or fabrication? It can be real, even if it cannot aspire to truth.

In this regard, my photograph is a key to my past, and not just in the testimonial sense that it bears an image of me—one that I no longer even have. My presence in the photograph attends to my absence from it. I see that I am there, but in doing so, I also recognise that I am not. It is a residual presence, much like a ghost. The nature of the photograph is partial trace, or perhaps more accurately, momentary trace. Viewing the photograph is a stark confrontation with my own absence from that moment in my childhood, and this disturbs me, firstly because it refers to my incomplete past. Like a fissure or a wound, it destabilises the sense of the collected whole. Yet, it also possesses an uncanny quality, suggesting something that is both present and absent, both tangible and immaterial, retrievable yet irrecoverable, permanent yet fleeting. In combination, these conditions form an invitation or perhaps more accurately a motivation. So I strive to recover the moment or the event, seeking to repair the w/hole.

The photograph is my key, unlocking this in-between space, this state of neither-nor in which I am obliged to attempt recollection, the most defining of human performances. I stitch my stories together, weave my webs, propelled by this feeling of discomfort, this unsettling in-betweenness, seeking the Gardens and an age where the things around me were free from labels or names, when like some form of jazz they existed in some wordless beauty. The truth is that the perfection of the whole past is inaccessible to us and my memories of this place are lost, but I can make something from the pieces, and while there is nothing that verifies every last fact, every last detail, perhaps stories are enough.

III

Zeami: "When there are secrets, the Flower exists; without secrets, the Flower does not exist."[4]

Recently, I was in Australia, where my travelling companion pointed to a tree trunk on which were carved letters, presumably initials, and the outline of a heart. It was an arrangement that seemed to contain personal relevance for me. Of course, I wasn't the author of this inscription, and hence it was impossible that we shared the same meaning. Thus, the carving announced the existence of a secret while protecting it at the same time.

Every now and then, one chances upon a tree with an inscription carved into its trunk. This happens anywhere in the world, any country, any setting, under any weather. As long as there are trees and people, sooner or later, people leave signs. Perhaps such carvings can be related to the basic urge to write or draw, simpler compulsions. Carvings are marks struck into the shape of the world, monuments that imply our presences in particular moments more than perhaps words and pictures—signs—alone, arguably more permanent or at least more physical in nature than the mere act of writing.

From my non-expert perspective, I supposed that the act of carving on trees would be a form of damage, but I understood that it poses a certain attraction because it is an act that partly announces, "I was here," while lending a great deeper personal meaning to the tree itself—this is *our* tree. By extension, this is our place, this moment belonged to us. Moreover, it is communicative. Sometimes there are initials, sometimes words, and sometimes symbols. Hidden in these carvings is meaning, not permanent, perhaps, and yet permanent enough. Typically, of course, these are indecipherable, like words announcing their presence to the vast sea. In the very best cases, one is able to guess their meaning using our shared pool of signs and by making reasonable assumptions—it seems difficult to misunderstand the symbolism of a heart-shaped inscription—but these are essentially unverifiable and none of these carvings can be syntactically or semantically deciphered with any degree of certainty.

One morning, I decided to catalogue these carvings, wherever they were, in the Botanic Gardens. Unfortunately—or perhaps fortunately—a combination of weather (again), good security, and poor eyesight meant that I only spotted two examples among the Gardens' many trees. I kept a record of them, nonetheless. Like all the other

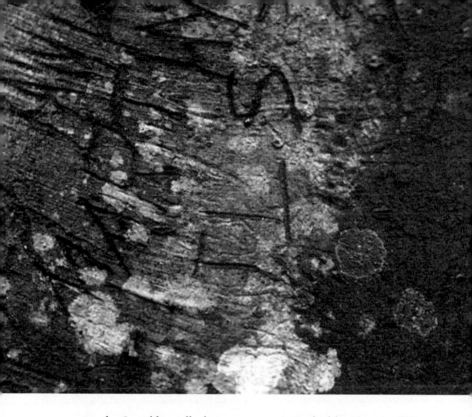

examples I could recall, these trees were marked by secrets, physically marked, these human signs impressed upon them by wilful
acts and twists of fate. Their silence vexed me, as if presented with
a lockbox without a key, with impenetrable codes but not the means
to crack them. I saw them as forms of memorialisation, but also as
wounds inflicted on trees. These carvings are scars, evidence of encounters between two very different domains. And much like these
carvings, scars are undecipherable to anyone without a shared history. That their meaning is often concealed only serves to reinforce
that our stories are like our/selves, that there is always more than
meets the eye, inaccessible to all except the closest of our confidants.

It is true that there is nothing original about this comparison, but there is some comfort in the thought that there are analogous existences in both worlds, trees and humans, different entities possessed by the same performance of life, of living, water and carbon, symbols and signs.

During the residency, I couldn't help but recall incidents of mild embarrassment in the Gardens. I remembered once avoiding the Gardens for an extended period of time after a particularly humiliating incident. I wondered if these incidents were the source of my discomfort or if they spoke of deeper insecurities. As I grew older, my odd and overly self-conscious view of the Gardens as panopticon, a place of surveillance, embarrassment, or trauma, gave way to notions of beauty and joy.

Perhaps my insecurities were telling. The garden is an impossible proposition, a creation of in-betweenness, perpetually neither here nor there, both this and that. A garden is neither manmade nor natural, neither stable nor inconstant, a physical space yet also an imaginary place, everything and nothing. It is a site of contestation between the abstract and the material, no, perhaps it is a synergy more than a contest. Perhaps this is the true beauty of the garden, and in my naïvety, I didn't realise that we are not often prepared for beauty, or that beauty disturbs us. And it is only in coming to terms with these discomforts, in identifying the true face of the garden, that I can begin to write.

As I write, I leave scars, traces. I walk down these paths, aware of the way that they trace the contours and shapes that comprise the Gardens, the way that they speak of geometries, defining and defined. I examine the old photos and pick at my brain for memories that I cannot remember, in search of lost meanings and thoughts from which to extrapolate, to imagine, and to resurrect. I examine these histories of scars to understand the ways in which reality leaves marks on us, and how we too leave marks in the world. I write in order to remember, no, to perform the memory, and through it, I work on this exquisite corpse, inscribing as one might on a tree, announcing the presence of a secret, yes, but also guiding you towards a meaning, which may belong to you or me, or perhaps is shared in the in-between. And so I compose, embracing the imagination and invention embedded deep within the nature of composition, and composition is the physics of reality. I create but also remember. Like growth and decay, like seasons and songs, it is cyclical. The writing reconstitutes remembrances, and the memories compel writing, and in this act, the only one available to me, I attempt to enact and examine the collision of two worlds, that of the self and reality around me, in search of the garden, the heterotopia, in search of the neither and both, because if we see the world in the garden, then it is a world of this overlapping destiny, a world of wood and of stone, of blood, of earth, of time, of recollection, of forgetting, of scars.

TWO ■ THE HALL OF ECHOES

I

In the photograph, I am standing under the orchid plant, the flowers
dangling slightly above my head. For some reason, I remember this

photograph very well, despite only recently having unearthed from among the other family photos. The frown on my face elicits laughter to this day. Behind me there is a woman, her back turned towards the camera, and beside her is a young girl, presumably her daughter, obscured by the plant above my head. To a side, there is a child in what appears to be her school uniform. The two children may be sisters or complete strangers. Who can say?

In the image, I am at an age without a sense of self. Or at least, I hardly remember anything of that period of my life, and in that case, it is difficult to say that I can count it as a part of my experiences. My mother remembers this scene much better than I do, of course—and very fondly too. She describes me as being so cute, which to me only underscores how entirely un-adorable I have become in the years since. I must be one or two, three at the most. There is a strange sense of the uncanny, for in confronting my early history, I am confronting a self that I don't recognise, one that I have to depend on externalities to confirm, or perhaps, in a slightly disturbing echo of the Lacanian mirror stage, it is revising my concept of self.

A photograph's physicality feels like an insistence. This seems contradictory. After all, in concept, all photographs are basically just assemblages of information, data, colours and distances and angles. This is even more pronounced in the age of digital photography, where everything is a matter of bits and bytes. The difference between a digital photograph and a physical print, however, is that the digital file is likely to survive for far longer than the object. This photograph has turned yellow, or maybe more accurately, a rusty colour, and the pigments have also faded, rendering the photograph indistinct and inaccurate. Forgive the easy metaphor, but it enacts the processes of memory in its existence. It seems inevitable to me that the day will come when the photograph will flake, will crumble. In this sense, there is very little that the photograph can retain. This thought is frightful to me, as if I will soon lose a part of me exterior to myself.

What the print insists on is not quite the contents of the memory itself, but rather that the memory has a presence in my world. A digital photograph sometimes carries with it a sense of immateriality and immortality, its nature sometimes hewing closer to data or fiction. The print begins as a record of the event, but as it deteriorates, it soon becomes a record not of what happened, but that something happened. It is thus a portal, or an invitation to remember rather than the remembrance itself. It is common to speak of the past as fixed, as a known quantity, and some are even fond of describing the future as predestined. But in a similar vein, if we accept that the future is characterised by unknowns, then we too must accept that the past is indefinite. It is filled with unrecoverable gaps and the dominant quality of uncertainty. Hence, the past is not so different from the future, and both possibilities are re/constituted in the present. The physicality of the photograph signals to me its place and its truth in the world, my world, my reality. If I lose its substance, then I lose the confidence that it exists or existed, and it seems likely that I will also lose its potential, the potential to imagine and recall.

I look at the photograph once again. The differences between its subject and me are so great that I cannot connect the dots. My face—no longer mine—is beyond my own recognition. And so I find myself having to rely on the word of my mother, the texture of the photograph, the information it contains, and the faith in the fact that everything seems to fit in logically. And thus for a moment, however briefly, I can imagine myself in those shoes, that costume, with a clumsy gait and a voice without words, standing under the clouds of long ago, and as I turn my head up, I see against the bright canvas of the sky the silhouette of orchids.

My family used to grow orchids in front of our flat. Growing orchids from seeds is particularly difficult. Orchid plants typically have a symbiotic relationship with specific types of fungi that enable them to germinate. This is necessary as the seeds of orchids, unlike those of most plants, do not store nutrients required for germination. I don't know what type of orchids they were, or where they had come from, but I remember them quite well. They were a part of our lives for several years, back when my dad was more physically active and willing to undertake extensive gardening. I distinctly recall thinking that everything about them set them apart from the other plants that we had growing in our small patch of HDB estate. They were planted in short, aerated pots filled with chunks of charcoal. The plants themselves also didn't look anything like our other potted plants, with narrow, seemingly segmented stems, exposed roots, and thick, waxy leaves.

I don't remember why we stopped planting orchids. I suspect that after a while, the outcomes were no longer commensurate to the effort that my parents spent maintaining them. Or perhaps they had simply become too much work. It is also likely that thieves had taken one or two of our pots away, which, as you can imagine, is incredibly demoralising. Like a David Lynch neighbourhood, the peaceful surface of mine conceals a seedy underbelly. Plant theft in my neighbourhood occurs with surprising frequency. Whatever it is, I tend to think that the end of orchid-growing for my family also signalled the end of an era. My parents would continue to grow a variety of other plants just as they would continue to give up on those that didn't perform as well—business as usual, in that sense—but the excitement and motivation that drove the careful tending of these plants would wane the moment they realised that they could not keep it up in the long term. After a series of failures and a number of thefts, my parents no longer had the time, energy, or motivation to continue at the same level as they had before. It was several years more before we would get to this stage, but that day my parents decided to stop cultivating orchids marked the beginning of the end.

Potted plants can still be found in front of our flat these days, but no orchids—and nothing particularly interesting either. We have a couple of small potted trees, bougainvillea, an unidentified and extremely leafy plant with slender branches, and a few other small specimens that spend their day not doing very well. There is a reason for this specific selection of plants: Crops—such as pandan leaves and chilli peppers—and the more uncommon or colourful flowers tend to attract thieves or vandals. This is not to say that I live in a bad neighbourhood, but the friendly aunties and uncles about are not above the occasional bout of petty theft, and even the most sporadic occasions of heartbreak were enough to render my parents tentative about the whole enterprise. Eventually, my parents stopped putting in significant amounts of time or effort into it, though that didn't keep them from conscientiously watering the plants, trimming the branches, and rearranging the pots. For a time, I struggled to understand their persistence with this endeavour because it made little sense to me why one would persevere with the effort when it was no longer rewarding. However, one day, I was compelled to help out with the gardening—lugging the watering can about, disposing of the trimmed branches—and it was then that I discovered the basic pleasure of simply getting work done. Perhaps integral to the concept of gardening is the concept of life giving life, or of lending extrinsic reality a human touch, but also crucial is the task, the routine, the practice.

I've never had much of a green thumb, but I would somehow carry on the orchid-growing legacy of my parents in a secondary school lab. When I was 15, I helped out in my biology teacher's research work along with a few classmates and would go down to the laboratory two or three days every week. By then, I was several years older, not wiser but at least much more aware of the nuts and bolts underneath the life of plants. The work mainly involved the maintenance of proper growth conditions for young orchid plants. These plantlets were housed in conical flasks of Pyrex. Many of those afternoons in the lab were spent working the agar in these flasks, a soft grey jelly-like substance that is nutritious for the young plants. The plantlets sat in the agar and over time, this substrate would decolour and degenerate into an even softer and slightly watery material, which was an indication that the nutrients had been depleted. Thus, it was necessary to provide fresh substrate each time, and we student helpers were responsible for this, transferring batches of young plants from one conical flask to another each time. The process involved putting on latex gloves, spraying 70-percent alcohol a little too carelessly, peeling off the aluminium foil covering each conical flask, and making the transfer before sealing each flask with parafilm.

There was also gardening to be done in the small yard behind the lab. I distinctly remember volunteering to do the weeding one afternoon. I didn't mind doing what may have been considered the menial labour in the lab and I suppose that speaks to my lack of ambition. I didn't ask questions. I just did as I was told. The work was simple enough and I felt happy to be a human-shaped instrument at the frontier of science. I also enjoyed being in that lab because it was one of the only air-conditioned rooms in school. Moreover, it was one of the newest and (partially as a result) one of the most advanced laboratories, though that probably isn't saying much for a group of boys who were 14 or 15. Which is to say that being in a biology laboratory was for me somehow associated with a misplaced sense of prestige. Being surrounded by smart people and interesting laboratory equipment certainly contributed to this impression. After all, it's not every day in secondary school science labs when you get to use centrifuges and autoclaves.

Furthermore, it felt like a place in which I could fit in, especially at an age where my sense of identity was still fragile—though I suspect this has not really changed much over the years. On the surface, I was doing my bit for the advancement of genetic science while amassing knowledge in a precious process of self-fashioning. In reality, I wasn't so much making the most of my secondary school education as I was busy hanging out with friends and earning brownie points. To be fair, there were far worse ways for an adolescent boy to spend his weekday afternoons, even if he didn't exactly make the most out of it. In retrospect, this time spent in my secondary school was really more of a type of social activity for me. I've never had the most smarts, but I compensated by trying to make friends with the best and the brightest. I believed that their brilliance would rub off on me and keep me afloat in those academically competitive years.

I also enjoyed the more routine aspects of my time in the lab. There was a sense of satisfaction in performing all the right steps to ensure that the environment was sterile, properly operating the fume hood, and even weeding the garden. While the meaning that I found in the work was limited, going down the checklist of things that had to be done would unfailingly give me a sense of accomplishment. It was the same feeling of satisfaction that I found when helping with the household gardening.

As I completed the tasks, I would think back to my parents' plants. I eventually concluded that in the various concordances of work and plant matter, it really was just another form of gardening, and that there is pleasure to be derived from the work.

As you might have guessed, our family is not especially gifted when it comes to plant matters. Neither of my parents was particularly talented in cultivating plants, and they didn't have the specialised knowhow to ensure that they grow well either. Whenever the weather turned or diseases struck, it often quickly became a matter of providence. Oftentimes, they couldn't even be sure why a particular plant failed to do well. What they lacked in gardening knowledge they made up for with effort and hearsay. However, there is a limit to what hard work and neighbourly advice can overcome. In short, we typically had no idea how well a plant would end up growing, or if it would grow well at all. Perhaps this should not be so surprising, because one can never truly predict the paths taken by each plant. In the end, gardening is an effort made to nurture each plant to its unknowable potential. It was thus that this comparison came to its full valance, and I saw that an arguably more crucial commonality was the nurturing of plantlets and the exploration of their possibilities, to ensure that they fulfilled their potential, and to see just what that potential entailed.

I spent many afternoons in that school lab, and in that setting, it seemed to me that there was something overwhelmingly mathematical and predictable about the entire process. Only later would I realise that we were not so far removed from Mendel's garden, tinkering away, trying things out, the rules of cause and effect still unclear.

It was within such a context that I eventually understood the hybridisation of orchids as a process of experimentation. No, in fact, the cultivation of plants in general is charged with a spirit of experimentation. While it would be too much of a broad stroke to associate the work of gardening with all forms of gardens, it is still reasonable to suggest that all gardens exhibit the same type of relationship with the future. For example, the research work of the Botanic Gardens— a segment of which has been orchid-related, no less—skews it towards the exploration of possibilities and fulfilling of potentials.

Orchid breeding in the Gardens became a major fixture partly due to the adoption of the family of plants in the nation's self-fashioning. Apart from producing hybrids and maintaining a sizeable population of orchid plants, the Botanic Gardens is as one might expect also invested in research into understanding the numerous species, and also the conservation and reintroduction of native orchid species in Singapore. The Botanic Gardens are also home to the National Orchid Garden, which opened in 1995. The garden houses hundreds of different orchid species and hybrids. One afternoon, a series of meetings was arranged to help me as I bumbled about attempting to complete my manuscript. One of the people that I met was David, an orchid expert and remarkable cultivator of orchid hybrids who took me through this garden.

David had a gentle demeanour and a grandfatherly air about him. He had a calm gaze and spoke in an exceptionally approachable way. We talked as we walked. I started with questions about things that I thought would be most useful in the completion of my writing, but the conversation proceeded in no particular direction for a while. David was happy to share with me all of his expertise, and in asking a variety of unrelated questions, I began to collect a series of facts. I learnt, for instance, that the orchids that we used to grow at home must have been a *Dendrobium* of some sort, and that they were popular back in the day as they grow easily. I learnt of the methods of growing different orchids, terrestrial or epiphytic. I learnt also of the classification of species, and the differences between them. I learnt that the prevalence of orchid hybrids is partly due to the large number of different orchid species that can be used as parents.

At one point, he explained to me the VIP orchid scheme, which I was familiar with, but it didn't hurt to hear it from an expert on the subject. Several are the orchids that have received the names of the famous. (Recently, David cultivated the *Aranda* Lee Kuan Yew.) Briefly, I wondered about the number of hybrids that have been cultivated and the challenges of cultivating them, which David was happy to elaborate on. When he went into detail about the different methods with which he tried to cross orchids, I realised then how unpredictable the entire process was. There is no real guarantee of success, and each cross can feel like a bit of a gamble in trying to produce a viable plant. When working to cultivate hybrids, effects may have invisible causes, especially in hybrids of hybrids where traits from grandparents can surface. I realised then that even at the most advanced frontier of plant cultivation, there was a substantial element of probability.

I also ended up learning more about him than I had expected. David told me about his Peranakan mother and how she used to cultivate roses. He explained to me that he began work on orchids after not doing too well with the roses himself. He also told me about how he originally worked in the shipping industry, and that cultivating plants was more a hobby than a paying job. Of the learning process, he said that he had to make many friends who would share with him their expertise in orchid cultivation. I couldn't help but think that he must have been one of the pioneering breeders of orchids locally.

During our meeting, David asked why I wasn't using an audio recorder of some sort. It was true that I spent my time scribbling away at my notebook or simply looking as though I was committing everything he said to memory. I wanted to tell him that I wasn't interested in the facts as much as I was in the stories, and that it is too easy to become obsessed with the small things, to allow the stories to be strangled by the minutiae of everything. I suppose I wanted to say that in a sense, I choose to forget, if only because it helps the stories from being totalised by the facts, the details. Yet, I recognise too the totalising effect of stories. I realised then that I was producing a superficial manuscript, a project that glossed over the substance of things. In any case, that didn't seem like the most natural of conversational options, and I elected instead to say that it was a habit for me to just scribble in my notebook, and also that I wasn't making a documentary. Shortly thereafter, when someone came to fetch me so that I could be chaperoned to the next meeting, David laughed and told her that he was just telling me stories.

It's true that I learnt quite a lot about orchids then, and yet I think David's personal stories left a deeper impression on me. One of the last things that David told me that afternoon was that the ones with passion are the sentimental ones. It became clear to me then how much the man loved the plants and the work that he undertook for them. I think back to that afternoon now, as the two of us walked through the garden of orchids, and I cannot help but feel that these plants attest to his work and the journey that he took to get here. While they remain silent, they testify, at least, to the fact that someone was here. Within them, one can see the shape of his mind, and the measure of the man who brought them into being.

Among the many orchid plants in the Botanic Gardens is an exceptional large Tiger Orchid that has recently been fenced up for its protection. This plant presents itself as a very messy bush—possibly home to a snake?—and I must admit that when I was first told of this plant, I wasn't all that impressed. It certainly lacked the soaring lines or fractal complexity of the great trees, the dramatic colours or quiet beauty of flora, and the quaint charm of some of the more unusual-looking plants. What a mess, I couldn't help thinking. It just seemed like a dishevelled or shaggy beast of an orchid, which is not quite what one tends to expect or want out of one's orchids.

I have gone back to see the orchid plant several times since then and let's just say that it has taken me quite some time to warm up to it. I appreciate it much better now. I suppose it has something to do with its history and exceptional qualities: It must be one of the oldest and largest orchid plants on the island, if not the world. Or perhaps it is because it looks so little like the types of orchid plants that I am familiar with. Or maybe, more simply, in its unkempt shape, it is hard to tell where it ends or begins.

It becomes clear to me that the Gardens—and indeed gardens in general—form part of the fabric of collective consciousness for Singaporeans. Singapore, after all, is sometimes known as the Garden City. Yet, the name is deceptive. In it, I find irreconcilable separation—disconnection, disjunction, dislocation. The term "garden" hides such complexities that sometimes it can only be dissimulation, disguise, refusing to disclose all of its truths.

Despite the name, gardening is not a major preoccupation of the average Singaporeans. Most Singaporeans live in a high-rise building—public housing or otherwise—and space is at a premium. One has access to perhaps the corridor or—if you manage to find a flat on the ground floor—a space that one might consider a very small yard, usually only enough for a row or two of potted plants, nothing too large or fancy. Besides, the very wet, rather hot, and extremely consistent weather in Singapore also means that some of the more colourful possibilities are impractical. It isn't wise to attract the attention of neighbourhood thieves and vandals with anything too conspicuous. To have a garden at home is therefore generally impossible in the residential areas—at least within the realm of public housing—and any attempts at the act of gardening can be rather limited.

Rather, the term can be traced to a tree-planting campaign launched in 1963 by then Prime Minister Lee Kuan Yew, which was then followed by the introduction of his "Garden City" campaign, launched in 1967 in part of a bid to comprehensively green Singapore. The Singapore Botanic Gardens would play a major part in this campaign, providing the required plants, research, and expertise. Over the years, the Gardens would prove to be crucial in realising the "Garden City" vision, and in various ways, it remains a major focus of the Gardens' work.

We are also a Garden City in more than this most direct sense. For example, the Botanic Gardens played a key role in the early stage of nation-building in fostering the racial harmony so crucial to the nation. Lee Kuan Yew officially opened the first edition of the "Aneka Ragam Rakyat" ("People's Variety Show"), a series of concerts staged in the Botanic Gardens. But more loosely, more diffusely, the Gardens is a place that people make memories in, a place that has collected and continues to collect the remembrances of Singaporeans. The garden is entangled in our histories—in both small and large ways.

Yet, the fact remains that the different facets of the garden—as archive, as scientific endeavour, as a place that protects the most fragile of possibilities—are sometimes difficult to locate in this country. Perhaps my time in the Gardens has left me aware that as a nation, we have created the physical garden, one that encapsulates the beauty of the centuries-old enterprise and partially the negotiation between humankind and the natural world but have yet to embrace fully its spirit and abstract complexities. We have constructed the space but have stopped short realising the fullness of its concept.

The national flower of Singapore is famously an orchid. The *Vanda* Miss Joaquim is a hybrid of *Vanda* hookeriana and *Vanda* teres. The plant stem is typically supported with a post and grows up to half a metre, while the flower is an exquisite blend of purple, pink, and white. It was named after Agnes Joaquim (Ashkhen Hovakimian), a horticulturist of some renown who cultivated it in 1893. Describing this particular orchid in an account in *The Gardeners' Chronicle* dated 24 June 1893, Henry Ridley, then director at the Botanic Gardens, wrote that "it is a very lovely plant, and is, I think, a great improvement on both the parents, beautiful as they are". Ridley also stated that the original plant was "now in the Botanic Gardens, Singapore, where it is being propagated by cuttings"[1].

The name *Vanda* Miss Joaquim is something of a misnomer. It was later discovered that both parents of this plant belong to the genus of *Papilionanthe,* and thus its actual scientific name is *Papilionanthe* Miss Joaquim, although it has retained the name of Vanda Miss Joaquim in common parlance.

It would be almost a century before the flower was selected as Singapore's national flower. In 1981, it was picked from a pool of forty candidates, the majority of which were orchids. David told me that it was the first registered flower hybrid from Singapore. Later, I would also learn that Singapore is the only country in the world with a hybrid as its national flower.

With the *Vanda* Miss Joaquim, Agnes Joaquim won first prize in an 1899 flower show. Unfortunately, only three months after, on 2 July 1899, she would pass away at the age of 45. Joaquim died of cancer, and her grave can be found at the Armenian Church along Hill Street. Visitors to her grave will also be able to find the orchid plant that bears her name.

Walking through the Gardens later that afternoon, I thought back to the naming of orchid hybrids, and lingered on the notion that these names contain within them a story of their creation but also of the people that they are named after. There is of course an Edenic echo in this, but more basically, these acts of naming contribute to the exhausting of possibilities, filling out the archive of permutations, checking the possibilities off the list one at a time. Our acts of naming are in this context acts of archiving, and in many aspects of the Gardens' work we can see the work of the archive. New species may be discovered, or species may be reclassified. The Herbarium in the Botanic Gardens also houses hundreds of thousands of specimens, and more are produced each year. The Library houses thousands of relevant books. There is also a shade of this in the production of botanical paintings, which the Gardens still engages in today. Each painting is not simply a description of a particular species, it is also a record of the subjectivity of the artist in a point in time. The Gardens were even at some point in their history also a (rather unsuccessful) zoo, and zoological gardens also contain within their conception an element of the archival.

With the veritable infinity of permutations of orchids, it's doubtful they will all ever be seen. Indeed, with each new hybrid, new possibilities occur. So perhaps "exhausting" is not the right word. We simply want to see what can be. The garden thus allows us at some limited level to stage the process of inquiry, of discovery, to see how our plants will turn out, or indeed what combinations are possible. If nothing else, the garden is an archive of natural histories, the stories of these plants, these names, these possibilities.

My mind wanders from this point to the flowering of the first orchid into the thousands of varieties today; to the experts in the Herbarium tracing the genealogies of species; to the great naturalist and evolutionary pioneer Alfred Russel Wallace, who would stay in

Singapore for some time as he did his research in the region, leaving behind some evocative descriptions of the island; to the sea, where all life begins, in the deep darkness of time, reality stirs. I think of the gravity that pulled all matter towards this instant, the invisible force behind each coincidence, each shift in the atmosphere, each chance encounter, every collision of particles. It is a game of chance, of probabilities. What precise series of events led to the first of the aerobic processes and subsequently the dominance of oxygen as cellular currency? What rains brought with them the sprouting of the first plants, or the enrichment of the soil, or the first sounds of life? I think of cells breathing their first, of worms tunnelling into ground and enriching the soil, of organic matter turning into fossil, into fuel, into the energy for which our civilisation thirsts. Nature, culture, language, meaning, all of it arising from a history of carbon, arising from a time when we were nothing but disparate atoms, unable to think, unable to imagine, and now, bound by coincidence after coincidence, taking a single path among so many, bound, that is, by a sense of singularity, one in the vast sea of possibilities, but the only that belongs to us. Cortázar asks: "Why have we had to invent Eden, to live submerged in the nostalgia of a lost paradise, to make up utopias, propose a future for ourselves?"[2] The answer is perhaps that it mimics our perpetual sense of loss, that we will never see the light of other days. Nevertheless, in its singular nature, this moment takes on the character of inevitable destiny. We were bound by the shadow of every turning to arrive at this instant, all natural histories combining to compose our stories, all possibilities condensing into this moment, into this ink, these words, this book, this codex.

II

On the same afternoon that I met David, I was also introduced to Elango, whose main work is arboriculture, the study and management of trees. It was the third meeting of the day, and by that time, I had become a bit winded. Thus, at the risk of sounding like a lazy person unwilling to do his own research, let me just say that I chose to let him lead the way. By which I mean I asked in the most professional manner possible: Do you have any tree stories?

To my surprise, Elango was game. I like to think that the question triggered something in him, because he then began to tell me a story of himself. Even though he supplied a few biographical details, he did so mostly by elaborating on some parts of his job. After we stumbled along a few tentative exchanges, he quickly gravitated to describing the parts of his work that he was proudest of. Elango took me around a good portion of the Gardens and showed me areas that he was working on. These areas were not usually obvious, although a construction site was something of an exception. During our tour of the Gardens, he pointed out to me Brazil Nut trees that he had planted, describing the way in which the mature trees would carpet the floor with their fruit and leaves in several years' time. He spoke of niches in which he would find space for new plants, and of larger trees creating the spaces in which smaller trees can grow. He showed me rare dipterocarps that he had painstakingly purchased, planned for, and planted in the Botanic Gardens. Someday far in the future—or maybe not even so far—this might be the only place to see these trees alive and well. I admired his vision, his ability to see several years into the future—that way of thinking on a different scale of time, one measured by the life of trees. The Chinese have a saying that forebears plant trees such that succeeding generations may stand in the shade.

Elango's passion for his work was palpable. With these examples, he described the most rewarding aspects of his job, which I understood as the planning of planting spaces in the Botanic Gardens. He talked about how it provides him with opportunities to plant rare trees, trees which may not even—probably won't even—survive in their original habitats. Whenever he broached this topic, the sense of urgency in his voice would be palpable, and I envied his deep belief in and commitment to his work.

Elango spent a long time with me that afternoon, and I felt bad that I was keeping him from more important work. I took away from the meeting several facts, but perhaps what was most striking to me was how silent, how invisible this story of a man with passion strong enough to shape these gardens so lucidly with the future in mind was. These trees quietly bear witness to his work. How many visitors to these gardens will recognise the species on the brink of extinction? or the care that underlies the layout of these lawns? But the Gardens are a physical record. One might even say that they remember, and through them, we remember too.

In our conversation, Elango constantly referred to the anthropocentric drive that motivates many of the decisions that one faces in
the public garden. It is a type of tug-of-war, or perhaps a matter of
pushing and pulling, to find the right in-between state. Elango elaborated on this as he told me of how he likes to retain an element of the
wild in the areas that he works on, so that it is not purely aesthetic
creation. It would thereafter be something of a refrain that he would
return to time and again. He would use it to explain, for example, the
symbolism of famous trees or the heritage of the Botanic Gardens.

Elango's words underscored to me that the garden stages the
intersection between humans and the natural world. While the subject of a garden is inevitably nature, a garden devoid of the human
mind is not a garden. And while I greatly appreciated his desire to
let things flourish naturally, it was also on my mind that the garden
began with human intent. The map of a garden is a map of human
ideas, human thoughts, human requirements, human definitions.
And perhaps what Elango identified in describing the constant push-
and-pull that characterises the design of the garden is also by another token an acceptance that there was an uncanniness to aesthetic
landscaping, a feeling of there-but-not-quite-there. But this in-betweenness is a key characteristic of the garden, and perhaps it is
from this perspective that we can understand it as a portal through
which to search for the human condition.

The Italian painter Giuseppe Arcimboldo produced several
paintings of human faces that were composed of objects following
a theme, often related to nature. These paintings were not the only

Giuseppe Arcimboldo, *Four Seasons in One Head*. 1590.

ones that Arcimboldo produced, although they are said to be his most popular. And he was also not the only artist to adopt this mode of expression. (Josse de Momper for instance would produce similar paintings with landscape painting.) Arcimboldo's paintings played on the well-known fact that humans will see faces in anything as long as the angles align, in a phenomenon known as pareidolia. The most famous example of this is probably the face of Cydonia, that image of a face on the surface of Mars. These paintings are in one sense visual puns, and without much subtlety too. By this I mean that they do not conceal their nature as puns, but rather insist first of all in letting you know what the game is. Sometimes it can seem as though that is their entire point, but on second thought, this is unlikely. After all, can one truly mistake an assortment of vegetables in an assortment of vegetable colours for an actual human face?

Among these paintings, I have always had a special love for the series based on the four seasons. These paintings have the plants and colours appropriate to each season configured into human faces. Roland Barthes characterised them as a "malaise of substance"[3], and perhaps this identifies the heart of the matter, that there is discomfort in seeing the human face where it isn't, substance where there is not. But this works both ways, for in our anthropocentric desire to see ourselves, we transform that which is substantial into the symbolic, the objective into the subjective. These paintings, in other words, explicate a sharing of states, undoing the clear-cut definitions that underpin the conditions of being.

These paintings succeed because humans are simultaneously

apart from and a part of nature. In search of humanness, we have othered ourselves from the natural world. Even the term "nature" is unfairly undifferentiating and brings to mind a reductive dialectic (man and nature). Perhaps we have continued to give names to species, to outline the order of the natural world, trying to locate our place in it. Or perhaps, much in the way of the first garden, it is a way of excluding ourselves from nature. After all, isn't the garden a place in which we can repeatedly exclude ourselves, consolidating our sense of self as human beings? This is reflected too in these paintings, for they too involve acts of classification and organisation, reflecting human thought and ideas of the relationship between all manner of things.

Arcimboldo's work comments on ideas of the dialectical relationship between humankind and nature by reminding us that we are never truly apart from nature, but also never truly a part of it. In disrupting the dialectic between the natural world and the human self, it also collapses the separation between them. This then is the lesson of the master, that while we may expend our energies in cultivating self-identity and fashioning our civilisations, in the end we are all made of the same matter, all carbon creations belonging to the same methods of organisation, existing in the same systems. We belong to the same reality. And perhaps all faces are masks and all people are illusions, all imaginings and impressions of the human mind. More than just being symbols for our faces, these paintings unmask us, and reveal that our faces themselves are symbols. These paintings also reveal that to the human mind, things exist in their immateriality, that all things become symbols and signs, images giving birth to more images. Imagine if you will a dusty and cluttered room. There, standing in the wan light, Arcimboldo stands painting, creating images speaking through images, pictures comprising each other, symbols referring to one another, as if to imply that to speak of a language with only the language itself is the first step in understanding our existence. Imagine the sly master of composite pictures, putting paint to canvas, convinced that our basic nature is facelessness—convinced, that is, that we wear our fictions for faces.

One day, I had a picnic with two friends on the lawn near the Swan Lake. It was a warm summer's day, as it tends to be in Singapore, but it wasn't especially hot and I could comfortably maintain a pleasant demeanour in front of my friends. We were celebrating my birthday, and as such I was told not to prepare anything. I arrived, as usual, too early, and, as usual, I went about taking photos. I remember passing by Holttum Hall, which has since become the Heritage Museum of the Botanic Gardens. When my friends arrived, we set up our picnic on a lawn near the base of a large tree. It was a very informal get-together and being complete amateurs, we didn't have a picnic mat, and had to pass our food around carefully while always keeping an eye on the ants. We also shared a bit of wine to go along with our snacks. The afternoon passed quickly, and it wasn't long before we had to go. As we were packing up, we noticed something of a commotion over at the famous five-dollar bill Tembusu tree to see her in quite some distress. A little girl was sitting precariously on the lateral branch of the national icon, too afraid to make her descent. It must have seemed like a good idea at first—happens to everyone. Naturally, her parents were panicking. Their daughter was crying loudly, the volume serving as a barometer of her distress. The incident, of course, attracted the attention of many visitors. My friends and I went over to see if there was anything that we could do to help, but we ended up just standing there agape. We didn't want to frighten the child even more, and it didn't seem likely that she would listen to our voices if she wasn't listening to her mother's. On top of that, none of us were especially adept at climbing trees, or confident that the branch would be able to take the weight of another person. Everyone stood by in a fluster, until she was eventually rescued by her father, who caught her as she courageously hopped off of the branch and into his embrace.

Later, I would learn that Tembusu wood is remarkably strong and that the branch is in fact so popular among visitors that people would clamber onto it in groups for photos when commemorating various life events from weddings to graduations. It seems almost miraculous to me that the tree has survived this many assaults on its physical integrity. Tembusu wood is famously hard, but there are few things more damaging to a tree than exuberant humans. A new support has been added to help the lateral branch build strength. There has also been a short fence installed around the tree which is meant to discourage people from climbing onto the tree, but also to keep human footsteps from causing soil compaction around the tree.

The tree's curved branch is arguably its most distinctive feature. Nigel Taylor, currently director of the Botanic Gardens, informs me that it is a sign that this tree grew on an open lawn, that is, without any close neighbours. This encouraged the development of a lateral branch that the wood structure was never

meant to be able to support. It is not the story that I expect, and yet it is a story nonetheless, one that explains how the tree came to be printed on money.

Every time that I take out a five-dollar bill, I find that instead of thinking specifically about the tree, I remember the little girl and her worried parents. The tree has become a symbol for me, and in that way, it is somewhat flattened, less material and more of an idea. To be fair, though, it had probably already done so for most Singaporeans the moment it was printed on the back of a note. One afternoon, I walked up to the tree, money in hand, trying to look for differences between print and plant. I was simply curious, but the effort was pointless and futile. At that point, I didn't realise that any actual differences between the illustration and the tree were meaningless. In my mind they were the same thing.

When I was a child, I was told that the age of a tree could be inferred from its tree rings. It was only much later that I would learn that this is something of an overgeneralisation. The phenomenon is the result of differential growth rates depending primarily on the weather. The density of wood in tree trunks in turn varies with the different growth rates, thus producing the visible differences between the inner and outer circumferences of each tree ring, which registers in the human mind as some sort of calendar. In other words, while it was still a good rule of the thumb, it is only truly effective in regions with pronounced seasons. This does not apply to trees in Singapore, where the two seasons experienced are monsoon and non-monsoon—sometimes haze and no-haze. The disappointment that I felt when I learnt about this truth behind Singapore greenery was crushing. It seemed to me that there was no longer any reliable method through which to determine the age of a Singaporean tree, but also because in being explained, the magic behind the tree rings had dissolved, the workings of wood clarified, as if the hidden meaning behind tree rings had been all but demystified. Or perhaps it is possible to think of it another way, that this intensified the mystery of trees. After all, can it not be said that instead of the progress of human years, the life of a tree could embody its own very, very long year?

Following these thoughts, I considered a question that had somehow never occurred to me before: What is the lifespan of a tree? Trees tend to convey stability and longevity, a certain lack of change, which if we are honest, is the true mark of an immortal. And while no one doubts that trees grow, that they change, that they wither and die, the history of a tree is charted on a different scale from the lifespan of a human. This stability might be one of the reasons trees pass quickly and easily into the symbolic realm. There is an old joke that has been passed around my extended family. It is the story of how my grandfather used to drive the family about, and he would navigate a particular stretch of road by using a distinctive tree as a landmark. Depending on the version of the story, either my grandmother or aunt would ask him: What will you do if the tree is one day removed? As you might expect, one day, the tree was chopped down and his landmark had vanished. In some versions, my grandfather would laugh nervously about it, while in others, he would turn grumpy. I don't think that there is any version in which he actually loses his way, but there is at least one in which he comes close. In any interpretation, however, the tree is unique to my grandfather. The tree is a *place*, or perhaps not even that—it is simply a *sign*.

Similarly, one afternoon, I walked up the path leading into the rainforest. I think I spotted the rather small and unassuming sign indicating the entrance and I couldn't remember ever being within the rainforest before. Thus, I began a minor trek into the woods. The rainforest in the Botanic Gardens is part of the greatly diminished natural heritage of the island, and I've been told that great efforts have been made to preserve it. I had no idea quite where I was headed and where I would end up, for the inside of the rainforest was shielded by the trees along its perimeter. Because it was a hot day, I was thankful for the shade and the fact that the air within the rainforest felt slightly cooler. The path was paved with wooden plants and diverged from time to time. I didn't think too much about where I was headed and spent my time struggling to take in all the details.

When I chanced upon the Johore Fig that stood midway along the path, I decided to take a break. I suppose "chanced upon" is a generous way of putting it. Having decided on one or two early turns, there was no way that I could avoid coming across the enormous tree. The other paths had closed. I have since been told that the Johore Fig is a type of strangler fig, which begins life rather precariously in the canopy of another tree. Once the fig is able to get a foothold, however, it begins to take in the nutrients that it needs to bulk up. Eventually, it strangles its host tree—hence the name—and proceeds to grow laterally. This, then, is how the Johore Fig in the rainforest grew to such a large size.

A squirrel decided to walk across the railing before leaping onto the branch of a nearby tree, but that was all the company I had in the twenty minutes that I spent seated at the bench. I sat there in its shadow trying to think of what I ought to do. I was not obliged to do anything at all, but as with many other things in life the lack of any action was disturbing to me.

I began to take photos of the tree, but was unable to capture its entirety, even within the frame afforded by my widest lens. To

be fair, I wasn't really thinking. I couldn't even see the entirety of the tree with my naked eye: of course there was no way it would fit within the frame of my camera. Eventually, I gave up and contented myself with abstractions. The roots were particularly attractive to me, and I was interested in the way that they were parallel and yet not quite so at the same time. Thus, I took several photos of small sections, without hope of ever stitching together a complete image. Then, when I was done, I sat down on the bench and looked up into the canopy, allowing the tree to take shape in my mind.

One Arcimboldo painting that I'm particularly fond of is *The Librarian*, a portrait of a man made out of books. It's possible to see this as either salute or satire, but surely the surface reading is that it is a metaphor that what makes a man is his archive.

One of the plays in Kuo Pao Kun's extensive oeuvre is called *The Silly Little Girl and the Funny Old Tree*. The play is about an old tree that people want chopped down. The tree is capable of communicating with a young girl, speaking in rather human terms about its state of existence. Unfortunately, but not at all surprisingly, the adults believe that this young girl is a kid doing kid things. After all, if the tree could talk so much, why did it only choose to talk to her? A series of dramatic turns ensue, and I believe—it's been a while since I've seen the text—the play has quite an unhappy ending.

The play may not rank among the most conceptually thrilling of Kuo's work, and I guess that might explain why I didn't like it at first.

I see it in a different light now, however, as I realise that it explicates the connection that people can have with trees in a delicate manner. It also emphasises the silence of trees, which is to say that the stories they contain—about themselves or about people—struggle to be expressed. Nevertheless, they are depositories of a sort, archives of a sort.

If the Botanic Gardens are an archive, then they are an archive of stories. There are stories that comprise its history and heritage, stories such as those that of the crocodile that ventured into Swan Lake; or of Tan Chay Yan, a tapioca planter in Melaka who was encouraged to plant rubber by Henry Ridley; or of Ridley's tree; or of a time when tigers roamed its woods; or the story of the King of Gambier. There are also stories about the plants and how they got here, how they became what they are today. Most of all, there are personal stories, stories such as David's or Elango's, stories belonging to every individual who has walked these winding paths.

All of these stories are interconnected, existing within an ecosystem, referring to each other, depending on each other. These taxonomies, these histories, and these anecdotes form part of the Gardens' substance, and through them we in turn access our own past, consolidating our personal archives, making memories, telling stories, performing our acts of remembrance.

If we are to consider memory in the garden, then we must accept that it is a record, sometimes silent, sometimes indecipherable, and that there are inevitably losses. But that is the condition of all remembrances, that nothing can be fully recuperated, and that things can be forever lost. With that understanding, the Gardens are a resource and an invitation, for here in the intersection of memories—historical, scientific, anecdotal, personal—every visitor becomes a detective, collecting clues, building cases, asking question, finding answers. And the gardens remain still, keeping their secrets, though sometimes affording as much as a whisper or an echo.

III

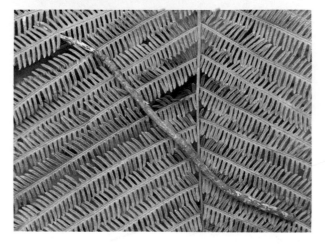

IV

Father tells me briefly that he remembers the Plant House the way it used to stand in the space that is now a small open courtyard. The structure was eventually removed because its integrity had been compromised by rot and nothing remains of it today. It was constructed in 1882 and used primarily for flower fests and exhibitions. Subsequently, it would house more exotic plants. I also read that it served as the backdrop for Malay royal weddings in films of the Fifties and Sixties.

Leading up to Plant House Annex is a set of brick steps. A bit of war history is concealed here. In 1942, the Pacific War came to the region and the Japanese Occupation of Singapore began. During this time, the Japanese took over leadership at the Botanic Gardens.

The British botanist Eric Holttum remained to advise the Gardens staff and was assisted by Eldred John Henry Corner, whose book *The Marquis* was recommended to me as one of the key accounts of the Botanic Gardens during the Occupation. These brick steps are an artefact from that age. Australian prisoners of war were tasked with making these bricks and to construct this staircase. It has been retained and one can still see the arrows on each of these bricks, marks that would denote them as government property back home, essentially a way for the Australians to stick it to their captors.

While it is difficult to know to the fullest extent what occurred in the Gardens during this time, we know for a fact that the Japanese were happy to allow horticultural work to continue. However, it wasn't all—to borrow a convenient cliché—a bed of roses, and it is known that a number of the outdoor staff were sent to work on the Siam-Burma Railway, in some cases at the cost of their lives. There have also been suggestions that executions took place in the Botanic Gardens during the Occupation.

Asking about the War and the Gardens, I was told about an incident that occurred during the construction of the current Botany Centre. One afternoon, all of the workers were too afraid to continue with the project, and upon being questioned said that the large tree within the construction area was haunted. An exorcist was called in and after performing his rites, he claimed that the tree was haunted by the casualties from the Occupation period. This tree is the massive Penaga Laut that still stands within the compound today. Within pockets of tranquil space, echoes of the War.

As a child, I was always highly excitable and easily frightened. If I'd seen anything that was colourful enough or macabre enough during the day, I was guaranteed to lose sleep in the night, unable to get it out of my mind. I was also easily spooked. I still remember—albeit not in clear detail—a time when ghost stories were popular across various forms of media in Singapore: There were informative programmes that took as their premise the unearthing of unexplained mysteries around the island; there were books of true Singapore ghost stories and articles about horrific murder cases in the nation's past. During this time, young as I was, I watched a Chinese drama series on Channel 8 comprising short stories of the supernatural. As I said, I was easily spooked, so it was probably not the wisest move, and yet, I couldn't resist. The appeal of the supernatural was too much for my juvenile mind. Besides, it wasn't as if I didn't think it through. It was simply that, against my better judgement. I was certain that I could handle it. After all, how scary could a low-budget local television production be? The truth is, it is in some cases extremely difficult to predict what will or won't frighten the living daylights out of a child, and I would soon learn that even the most absurdly clichéd depiction of a ghost had the capacity to make me lose sleep.

This particular episode featured the story of an older woman who died under less than pleasant circumstances and thus became a ghost. The actor who played the ghost put on some dreadfully ashen makeup, coloured her hair, and dressed up in white robes. I seem to recall that her performances tended to be ridiculously hammy and her voice was always modulated so that she could make spooky echoes. In all, it was a very trite representation of a ghost in a genre with more than its fair share of tired clichés.

There is almost nothing I remember of the plot, but for several days after I was haunted—as one is tempted to say—by the image of the old lady howling on a stormy night on a plain with a solitary frangipani tree, accompanied by flashes of studio-manufactured lightning. The leaves on the ground swirled with the studio-manufactured wind to hammer home the drama. Through the magic of editing, the old woman teleported all across the screen. One moment she was to the left of the screen, then far behind the tree, and then all too suddenly, she had her face buried in the camera. Nothing about that was actually frightening because it was all too transparent. Rather, it was the *idea* that there could be and probably was a vengeful ghost attached to each tree that really scared me.

At that age, I struggled to put the images out of my mind because of the way they connected to my world. I could no longer shake the possibility that there were ghosts waiting for me the next morning behind every tree. I spent almost the entire night awake, trying to forget the face of the old woman who had terrified me through the television screen long before Japanese horror came into fashion. Of course, the more one tries to forget something, the deeper it is cut into one's memory. It didn't help to remember that I knew perfectly well who the actor was, that she was in a host of other drama serials, and that she was most definitely not a ghost.

There was and still is a row of frangipani trees near my block, and for a number of years I deliberately avoided walking along that path. When I could not avoid it, I made sure to skirt around the flowers that had fallen onto the path for fear of being cursed. Bear in mind that I was only eight or nine years old, and at that age I was quite superstitious about things because there were so many things that were frightening to me, including scarily lit ladies in pasty white makeup.

Time eventually robbed me of my fear of haunted plants and I would also soon lose my timidity and superstition as far as matters of the afterlife were concerned. My fascination with things dead or dreadful, however, has remained. I reckon this has to do with the sense of mystery that is attached to these stories, that even at their most disentangled they resist solution and resolution. I was also fascinated by their unusual state of being, neither alive nor truly dead. Perhaps it is appropriate then that trees play a key role in a number of ghost stories, for trees exist in a state of in-betweenness as well— they are a place and yet not quite a place, always changing yet exceptionally stable, substantial and yet symbolic.

Frangipani trees, or plumeria, have something of an unfortunate connection with the supernatural in this region. The Pontianak, for instance, is the ghost of a pregnant woman in Malay and Indonesian mythology that is supposed to reside in banana trees. It is also said however that she lures victims with her attractive figure and her presence is said to give off the fragrance of the frangipani at first. Much later, I learnt that Paul Theroux wrote that the Pontianak may simply be an invention of wives trying to scare their husbands off of extramarital sex. But at that age, what did I know? And besides, what could Paul Theroux possibly know? I was perfectly justified in treading lightly to avoid offending the spirits so unhappily bound to these beautiful trees.

As I said, however, I began to realise that my childhood fears were completely unfounded when I grew older, and that there was perhaps some truth in Theroux's words. That said, I continued to find the idea of ghosts fascinating. I realised then that there wasn't so much to separate ghosts from other people. Besides, surely if I were to become one, I thought, I wouldn't want to be stigmatised by the living. It is true that one can expect there to be vengeful ghosts, but one can also expect vengeful people in life as well.

Indeed, as I became more and more aware of the human inevitabilities of love and loss, I began to come to a different understanding of why ghosts have such a grip on our imagination. It wasn't because they were dangerous or mysterious, but rather that ghosts, like stories, pictures, are expressions of memory. Ghosts exist because of us. They participate in our cultures and are created by our remembrances.

These days, I remain haunted, although I've never seen any ghosts for myself. The closest I got was seeing a mysterious shape on the running track late at night in secondary school. Admittedly, my life would be rather different if I'd seen any actual spirits, but the ghosts of memory are arguably more difficult to avoid. They return time and time again, these images and impressions, these immaterial shapes, these spectres, these shadows.

Recently, I found myself back in the same area having to take some photographs for friends. Quite foolishly, I agreed to help my friend out by taking some photos for her wedding. Having failed to prepare adequately for the occasion, the pressure was on. We had something of an itinerary and it included an early morning stop at the Botanic Gardens. The couple sought sites that were meaningful to them. I can only surmise that those were places that they had spent time together before, although I asked no questions and for all I knew, they chose those spots simply because they liked the scenery.

I enjoyed the experience, but I did feel as though I was intruding upon something. I reckon this comes up for every photographer who has to deal with people. It feels voyeuristic when the subject is unaware of your presence, and intrusive otherwise. The photographer must exist primarily as an outsider. Throughout the day, I watched as the couple shared a private connection. What did these trees mean to them? Why were they laughing when they got to this spot? I was an outsider who had to pretend to have insider knowledge, but really, all I was doing was trading in the familiar tropes of romance and praying that it would be enough.

While the photos were in no way exceptional or even professional, I constantly reassured myself by thinking that there is something of a personal touch to them—and maybe that was the reason the couple asked me to do it in the first place. As I looked at the photographs, however, I couldn't help thinking that there was something clichéd about the whole endeavour. Soon-to-be married couple posing for pictures in the Botanic Gardens? Sweet as it was, it was hardly

the most original idea. And yet, can something so personal truly be considered clichéd? During the session, I was privy to a connection hidden from the rest of the world. I could see hints, shades, sketches of shared experiences and remembrances of things past. I was an outsider but I had also been allowed in. I was in two places at once.

Some days later, I would return to the Gardens to attend the wedding of the couple. I knew nobody else at the wedding and as such it was a rather stressful occasion for me. I felt outside of proceedings, exterior to the event despite being a guest. It was like failing to grasp an inside joke. And yet, in spite of this distance, I knew that in one or two small ways I had participated in their union, and even if the enacting of romance in these gardens draws upon tired symbolic currency, they give shape to more delicate meanings under their veneer.

Mother tells me that when they were dating, my parents liked to hang out at the Botanic Gardens. She says that they never really stepped into the Gardens and stayed in the area just outside of Tanglin Gate, towards the hospital, where they would have dinner for movie nights. She fondly refers to the satay and roti john, and I can only assume that those were the more popular of hawkers there then.

My mother is at a phase in her life where she likes to repeat stories whenever opportunities present themselves. I've grown used to it, and I typically enjoy hearing about my parents' dating past. I suppose that in a cheeky sort of way, it is searching for the story of how I came to be. When she heard about this project, she quickly volunteered this bit of trivia, and while the details are sparse, I appreciated hearing about it time and again. I'm not implying that I don't think my parents still love each other today, but it's difficult to imagine my parents young and in love. That is, perhaps because of my belatedness within their lives, I've never been able to imagine between them the sort of romance that one enjoys in one's youth, the sort that bears a certain nervousness or a certain sparkle. Maybe this is simply a way of saying that it is difficult to imagine my parents young again. These days, I accompany them to their medical appointments. These days, conversations are not quite about the things we remember but rather the things that we struggle to remember. These days, I begrudgingly accept the brevity of our lives.

There are no photos of these dates that my mother tells me of. People like to document their memories and my father is no exception. However, most of the relevant photos I have managed to un-earth from the family albums feature my parents on the lawns of the Botanic Gardens in the daytime, most certainly because of the tech-nical challenges of photography when light is at a premium. I also imagine that in an age before the ubiquity of consumer cameras and camera phones, it was probably unbecoming to be snapping away when out with your date. As a result, I have very little with which to corroborate this story. Not that I doubt my mother's words, but sim-ply that it is too difficult to imagine what it would have been like.

I returned to the same gate time and again, as though standing at the very spot where my parents spent several evenings would help me to reconstruct the scenes in my imagination. Each time I tried to fill in the blanks, to sketch in my mind the faces, the fires at each stove, to tune my ears to the echoes of days long past, to catch even a whiff of the scent of the food that she tells me of; but everything is too vacant, possessed by the tone of fiction. Nothing is availed to me, nothing connects me to the past. I return to the place repeatedly try-ing to sketch her account in my head, but my efforts amount to little more than flits and flashes. I'm not even sure if the Tanglin Gate has moved since in the first place. Nevertheless, futile as my efforts are, I find that I cannot resist trying. There is nothing for me to return to, no sight, no sound, no shadows, not even an echo.

The Botanic Gardens are said to be a favourite spot for dating cou-ples, although I have neither the facts nor the experience to testify to this. There is something about gardens in general that renders them conducive to romance, and the Botanic Gardens are no exception, a fact which goes back decades. The lawn where I toasted to friendship with my buddies may be good for picnics, but it was also where, I'm told, men and women from respectable families would be introduced to each other. These days, one is more likely to see couples having picnics or simply sauntering along on this lawn.

Another popular romantic location is the Bandstand, where couples on the verge of marriage vows sometimes end up queueing in full dress just to have their photos taken. This distinctive gazebo was not always a feature of the Bandstand area. While it was the location of musical performances even in the earliest days of the Botanic Gardens, it was only decades later that the familiar octagonal structure would be constructed. There are several photos of Mother and Father

here, from what seems to be an early time in their relationship up to a later period where even my sister makes an appearance.

Eager to pursue the love story of my parents, I consulted the family archives, which is a dramatic way of saying that I flipped through some old photograph albums. I found several pictures of my parents in gardens of some sort, and quite a few that I recognised to be in the Botanic Gardens. To see these old photographs is to be confronted by their punctuated nature. They do not have much in the way of narrative, or even information. In a way, the memories that they contain are already forgotten, and yet they remain with a defiant permanence. It's possible to recognise photographs from the same series based on the places and the clothes, but the staccato nature of this photographic archive remains. These are images plucked from time, so limited in information, so barren of context that they require an active reconstruction.

Faced with this void, I attempt to identify patterns across the photos. The most obvious one was that of Mother posing in the same way at the same tree in a few different photos. In these images, her hair is puffier, in a manner of speaking, somewhat like her blouse, but she doesn't look as different as one might expect. She verified that these pictures had been taken in the Botanic Gardens, although, somewhat to my disappointment, she said that there was nothing special about the tree—she just liked posing next to it. That should have satisfied my curiosity, but it didn't, and I wanted to see it for myself. And so, in search of Mother's tree, and indeed her youth, I walked the paths of the Gardens over and over, trying to catch a

glimpse of a matching shape. I knew deeply that this was a futile enterprise. What were the chances that I could locate a tree decades removed in the present day? What were the chances that the tree was still there? I knew that I wouldn't find her, that woman in the photographs, standing next to her favourite tree. I was searching for an image, something that *did not exist*, and so, in the moment that I gave up on my fruitless quest, I said to myself very quietly, Mother is nowhere, Mother is gone.

In 2013, I was dating a girl from Hunan who had come to Singapore to do her PhD. It was an ungainly sort of relationship, neither of us too certain of where we were going or what we were going to do. Unfortunately, being as clumsy as we were, it ended very poorly. The relationship didn't last very long, even if I tried very hard to make it work— perhaps I tried too hard. On the day she brought it to a close, it felt as if a great rift had developed imperceptibly and it was already too late to salvage our relationship. She texted me that perhaps we should remain friends, but even that promise seemed too much to live up to and we never spoke again.

I remembered a day when we had spent a long evening with each other and, approaching midnight, found a garden swing in the heart of the central business district. It was painted in silver and reminded me of one that I used to jump onto when I was a child. It was early in our relationship (our first proper date, in fact) and late in the night, and I recall being extremely surprised that she was willing to indulge me and miss the last train home. We wandered around the city centre, where I showed her some of the landmarks. We also managed to watch people flying their brightly lit kites along the Singapore River. She did most of the talking during this time. Eventually, we came upon a garden swing standing in the middle of the central business district. Something about its out-of-place nature encouraged me to seize the moment, so I put my hand on her wrist and led her to it. We sat there for close to half an hour, having somewhat run out of words to say, tired but contented.

One day when I was aimlessly wandering in the Botanic Gardens and I chanced upon a group of frangipani trees planted seemingly equidistant from each other, my eyes were drawn to the garden swings that stood amid them. I couldn't resist climbing onto one of them. And it was in this, a miniature forest of plumeria, that I sought my own ghosts. I sat alone for what must have been close to half an hour. The silence around me was intense, almost suffocating. I could feel time passing, but a different time, one that belonged to that distant evening when I could still hear her voice, but also my own.

I stood up and walked among the trees at a deliberate pace, still lost in thought. My mind was in two places at once, returning to that night but also wandering in this spectral forest. Lost in my memories, and sometimes barely even memories, just echoes, the sounds of former love, the past bled into the present, one leading to another, coming full circle. There I wished I could speak to her again, to apologise, perhaps, to thank her, to say the things

that I had neglected to say. I could picture it, almost being able to speak to her again, almost being in that same moment, almost being as intangible and false as the image of her that I had conjured. It was as Derrida once said in that film: The ghost is me.

We return time and again in search of lost times and lost spaces, and so it was that I found myself almost as if in a dream. The lines were indefinite, the voices hollow, but if I could not be back in time again, at least I could have the illusion. We return time and again to places and thoughts seeking lost loves and loved ones lost. And perhaps this is our condition, strangers in the hall of echoes, desperate for that which cannot be returned. Ours is a condition of mourning. It was also Derrida who said: "We must, but we must not like it—mourning, that is, mourning itself, if such a thing exists: not to like or love through one's own tear but only through the other, and every tear is from the other, the friend, the living, as long as we ourselves are living, reminding us, in holding life, to hold on to it."[4]

We depend on each other, rely on each other to construct our existences, but we are equally marked by appearances as we are by disappearances, presences as absences. For in every union, and every friendship, every single human encounter looms the spectre of parting, and also the spectre of death. I realised this as I searched for you and saw you in the Gardens, approaching, then turning your back, then departing. There was silence for a moment, and that was all that was availed to me. Not your voice, not your words, not your touch, not even your face. And in that instant, you were my secret, you were my lie, you were my poem, you were my song. I didn't go after you. I didn't call your name. I only stood and stared at your vanishing figure, and the space of my mind contracted until it took the shape of a single word: goodbye, goodbye, goodbye.

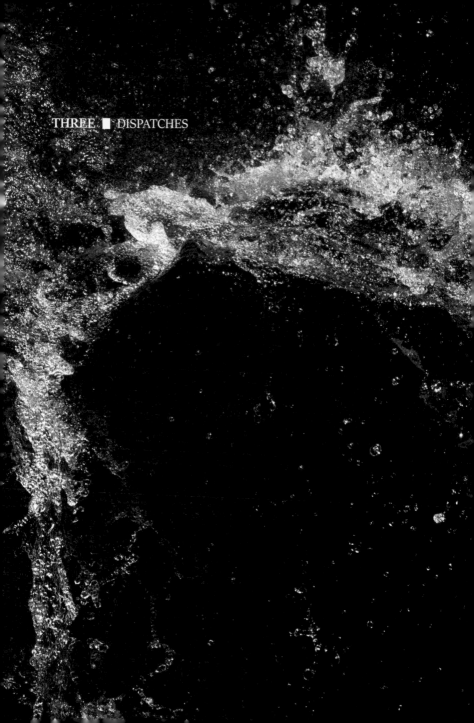

THREE ▌DISPATCHES

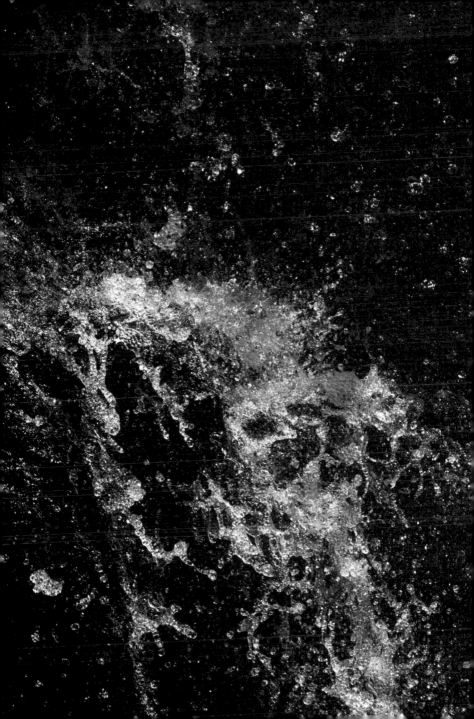

I

Every moment is soundless, every instant a silent admission that reality barely exists in stasis. This is how I conceive of the Gardens, an instant that blossoms in search of you, and yet also poised with you as its point of origin, its plan, map, mandala. In the beginnings of my fabrication—for all writers are fabricators, craftsmen, fiction-makers, liars—there is only the instant, and in the instant, nothing fades, nothing appears, and nothing changes. Nothing happens. Nothing travels. Everything is there, but simply still. In the moment, the swans are motionless, the birdsong sits in suspension. In the stillness, everything is primed to travel from one moment to the next, but in the instant, nothing travels. But this is a concession, for if we are to imagine a single droplet of water failing to descend, frozen but not ice, surely we also imagine it shimmering in the sunlight, reflecting, refracting. In this we read a greater problem. The Gardens should reach us in the manner that light reaches us, like the sea, a constant play of waves and currents, travelling through space and down nerves, but if it is true that nothing travels, then not even waves do, not sound, not light, not the electric currents that carry sensations through the body and to the mind. That is to say that the instant is a vacuum of information, devoid of context and connection. In the instant, nothing is known. Words are halted and meaning is impossible. Space becomes constricted, the dark emerges, expanding, until its meaninglessness—or perhaps its absence of meaning—totalises the reality that we recognise, to which we belong, that we have made. Subjectivity collapses with no subjects and no possible subjection. And if nothing changes, if nothing can change, then reality is stripped of its necessary entropy. Hence, time sheds its condition, stretched, thinned beyond all recognition. Perception too is rendered impossible. The instant is deprived of data: there is nothing to know, and knowing is impossible. Without the possibility of light, darkness becomes meaningless. It does not even have the meaning of absence. I have started with an idea of the Gardens, flawed, fraught, frightening. Thus into silence, thus into obliteration, into darkness, no, nothingness, not gravity, not space, not time, no.

But this is not the instant. Ours is a universe of connections, forged, enduring, broken, lost, missed, and if we are to believe in its substance, if definitions of time are to remain viable, then the instantaneous always occurs in the turning of the moment—each instant is always a part of a series of instants. Thus I fashion these Gardens again in the space of my mind, until it overtakes me, becomes the space of my mind. So it is that in imagining a precise point in time, we affirm its participation in a history, in a progression of moments, in an unreadably complex web of causes and effects. I know that every moment is not simply a moment but the possibility of different moments. And just as every person is a citation of a culture or a civilisation and every tree is a reference to our natural histories, every atom implies its universe.

I build again. I begin to weave together these paths. I sculpt the trees into shape, form the rigid shapes of buildings, fill in the shades of colours. Just listen and you will hear the flutter of small things, the groan of summer, and perhaps even the humming of the universe. And I fill in the intangibles—the glimmer of the sun on the water, the shadows—and the invisible—the taste of the air, the chorus of insects, the textures, growth, respiration, the photosynthesis of each plant, each luminous machine. And so it is, atom by atom, molecule by molecule, the Gardens are made again, every particle vibrating, colliding, its position uncertain, indeterminable.

This indeterminacy is what I seek. For decades we have known of the uncertainty in quantum systems, that the more information we have of a particle in any given dimension, the more it restricts our knowledge of it in the others. We can never really know where each electron is at any given moment in time. But with this limit to our knowledge there is a proliferation of probabilities. This is also our natural condition in the world. It is impossible to know all things, to describe all things except in the vastness of possibilities, where every space can contain a myriad of overlapping states. And in this indeterminate reality, the moment emerges from the void, begins to bloom, revealing the structure of all matter. Only thus do the Gardens begin to exist. This microcosm is but one in a sea of possibilities, and yet it also articulates a measure of inevitability, a sense of destiny, for I began from a single point, I began by looking for you. In search of you, I fabricated the Gardens anew.

These Gardens are exterior to me. They exist only in my mind, but they are removed from me. To know them, I am compelled to wander their paths. So I awaken, choosing my face, sculpting my voice, speaking, breathing, formed and deformed, shaped and misshapen, somewhere in between. I am fashioned in the interstitials, in the spaces with no name, and I become keenly aware that every atom bears your name, every sound carries the tenor of your voice. From stillness, from the frozen time, the Gardens bloom. From you, from your absence, I created this space of overlapping possibilities, this impossible moment, our mutual utopia. My writing is not merely an object, but a path, and with the faith that it will inevitably lead me to you again, I walk trails paved with fallen leaves and forgotten rain, perhaps just to see you again, perhaps just to say hello.

II

Perhaps you don't remember the day, the pocket of time, the miniscule space in which we existed. You and I exist only in that place and that time, two souls concealed, protected by the dark. Never before and never again.

I decided to write her a letter. (Derrida: "I would like to write you so simply, so simply, so simply.") There were things that I didn't know how to say, things that were difficult to pin down. I supposed the only recourse for me was to find out by writing. I thought so when I first began to write the letter, and I maintained the same thought draft after draft. Even now, when the letter has been sent, read, and replied to, it feels incomplete. I wrote over and over again in search of impossible words.

Or perhaps I chose to write a letter because I was never couldgeous enough to speak. Writing is my chosen form not because I am any good at it, but because writing generates something irreducible. I also chose the form of a letter because I wanted to maintain the possibility that a letter does not arrive at its destination.

It's no use. I can't really remember that evening in the Gardens. That is, the details that enter my memory are too few. Too little substance and too much void. I have no photographs of either of us from that day. The camera felt intrusive the moment she appeared.

The words are raw, rough-cut, unhewn. I've read them several times and have come away with the same impression each time. When I first wrote them, I knew that they were unfinished, and even through several drafts, I kept them the same way. I'm not sure why this is so, but I can hazard a guess. I think I felt the urgency of the matter—which is ironic, considering how I chose to resort to a letter—and knew that I had to write quickly.

More importantly, however, there was the idea of the work-in-progress. That is, I liked that it was unfinished, to leave enough space for more words, future words, possibilities, potentials.

Time has sculpted the memory into something pristine, into something too vague to be imperfect, and I am afraid that anything other than silence would be too vulgar for its delicate shape. I have avoided talking about it, writing about it, because its haziness protects its amorphous nature, keeps it without shape, like a text before it is written, open to all the possibilities of the imagination. I have avoided it until, of course, today. Perhaps I can finally remember it in a way that does not dissatisfy me, or at the very least, perhaps I can find the courage just to let it be.

The day gave way to darkness much faster than I had anticipated. Before long, we became voices in the dark. The Gardens was tinged in the familiar orange of Singaporean street lamps. It was still quite dark, however, and I found that it was necessary to reconstruct the Gardens in my mind. I suppose I had wanted the night to go on for as long as it could, and in my mind, I thought of Cortázar, who wrote: "I realised that searching was my symbol, the emblem of those who go out at night with nothing in mind, the motives of a destroyer of compasses."[2] We walked in the darkness, having run out of conversation topics to unspool. The day had run its course. All that was left to do was to see it out. Thus, we strolled down paths now less familiar, fully intending to call it a day. We had a vague sense of where we were headed and the certainty that all paths led to the outside. I remember that you asked about my accent and I told you that I don't really know. I must have deployed the same old joke that I always use, that I had watched too much television. In my mind, I was thinking that it, like all other things that night, was a performance in any case, perhaps a subconscious or even an unconscious one, but a performance nonetheless. Unfortunately, I don't remember anything else that was said. Instead, I only recall struggling to recite in my head Valéry's words, which, in that moment, were the only words that I managed to recall: "We are nothing without one another and yet between us is pure abyss."[3]

I returned to the Gardens recently one afternoon. I think I found the tree under which we sat, but I couldn't be sure of it. Of course, we already know that my memory is hardly outstanding and there is very little that I could be certain about in the first place. Furthermore, accounting for growth and decay, landscaping, and other factors, it was in fact impossible for me to have identified it. I simply assumed that I found the right tree. I sat there again on the slope. It didn't afford me any shade, but I wasn't intending to spend too much time there. I sat on the grass and stared at the stage. The sight of it was so unfamiliar to me. I ventured to take a photo although it did not prove very successful. In the end, I was not interested in reliving memories or any pretensions of reminiscence. Rather, it just felt like something I should do. Perhaps it was an act of memorialisation.

Sometimes, the sun is a tyrant, its incomprehensible light serving to unearth our memories but laying to waste our remembrances at the same time. Daylight, in all of its intensity, has the ability to eradicate or destroy. It is only in the shadows that the delicate can thrive against the sun.

After the sun sets, it leaves behind emptiness. Perhaps it is unfair to describe the night as emptiness. The night is more comparable to dark matter, an invisible presence. While we are quick to recognise the absence of light, we fail to see the settling darkness. The night brings certain assurances. It is both the realm of sleep as well as the domain of dreams. Dreams tug at the cloth of the world we make in the daytime, revealing its true face by disavowing its mechanisms. Through dreams, we usurp the senselessness of logic, we abandon rationality—we embrace the gloaming so that we may exist.

This is the invitation of the night, one to shield and enshroud that which cannot bear the cruel opacity of day. And so I thought at that moment that we walked down its paths, sheltered by the darkness, that surely, for all of our lives, we will have the day and its colours, the brightness of morning and the heat of the afternoon. We will have both swelter and storm in these gardens once termed the gardens of eternal summer. Certainly, the sun is the force that drives nature and creation, the blossoming heart of the garden, but the night is its human soul. And so it was made plain to me that just as the day speaks in certainties, the language of night is that of possibility. For surely the light is that which gives life, but only the night is amenable to fragile things, and within it, we search for sorrow, longing, and perhaps love.

We are older now, our bodies bearing the scars of the living and our minds having accrued the experiences and experience of years. We are older now, and I would like to think that we have changed along similar paths, and perhaps that has brought us somewhat closer together. Wishful thinking, I know. Three years have passed since the evening in the Gardens, and they have been a complicated time. I had hoped that it would help in trying to bridge the gap between the two of us, but I know that the distance between us has only deepened. I am other to you, an outsider, and will perhaps remain so.

But at least, for this moment, at this time, I have the night, and it is indefinite, uncertain, inviting. In the night, I have the memory of you, the echo of you, and through it, the memory of us. And so I remember, again and again, before my time is up, the two of us walking together along the paths of the Botanic Gardens, towards the gates. And I remember the safety of the night, however fleeting, and how reality beckoned, the exterior world forcibly intruding upon our consciousnesses. It was thus that our evening came to an end, as we emerged from the gates, and there was no question that it was still night, but leaving the Gardens seemed to return us to the inevitability of the morning light. Which is to say that as we crossed the gates back into the city, there awaiting us was the promise of daybreak, and so we entered the city, two souls in parallel, two worlds doggedly apart, returning to days of too little darkness, or too much light.

III

In these Gardens, I find traces of myself from all stages of my life, traces that I've failed to remember and traces I will never forget. In these Gardens, I am disturbed, enchanted, injured, inspired. In these Gardens, I fell, and I fell in love. Perhaps what I seek is a way of both leaving things behind and taking things with me, to selfishly decorate these trees in scars but to also carry the scars within me. Perhaps I leave these words as portals to stories and histories, in the hope that they will be deciphered, that they will speak to someone willing to listen. I wrote of the Gardens to begin writing of the Gardens.

Every moment is soundless, every instant a silent admission that reality barely exists in stasis, but in writing we carve paths to walk on. This is my letter to you, a love letter that mourns what was and what could have been, an invitation to this garden of indeterminacy, this city of hybridity, a confession, an archive, a photograph of this moment that we share. It was you, you who I fell in love with, you who defined the shape of my mind, you who are my garden, my city, my song, because only with you can this codex begin to speak. And every sentence is an injury, each word a scar, but I carve them into a consciousness that we share, inviting pasts and futures, ghosts and fantasies. This is nothing more than a letter, an object, a text, and yet, and yet, a letter never ceases to stop speaking, never ceases to create, not an object but a process of making and remaking. And I write because I don't know how to leave you. I write because there are no words to write with, because it hurts to think of a time when I will be removed from the possibility, however slim, that we may together inhabit a world in between. I write because I know that we may share a space but not a place, a time but not a moment, that even as we stand face to face, our gazes meeting, our hands almost touching, we are still unable to share the same rain. So it is that as I slowly let go, or perhaps that it gradually slips away from me, this codex protects, continues to protect, before it is lost forever, a universe and its darkness and silence, a distance overcome, the never-night in which you respond to it, saying yes, perhaps yes, yes.

MOTHS

■ Scars

2017

[1]

One day, I will no longer remember you, no longer be able to remember you, but I will always bear these scars.

You told me the scars on your leg were the result of a childhood cycling accident. You were riding with your mother when it happened. You bore the mark of the trauma but your mother bore the burden of guilt—the telepathy of scars.

I was unable then to tell you that our scars are inscriptions beyond linear time. I didn't understand it at the time, but I know now that our scars are our stories, a resistance against effacing change but also the change themselves. These stories, these images, these sounds, they are the archives but also the scars. They mark our disconnection from places and our connection to others.

[2]

My grandmother suffered a fall in 2016 and was admitted to the hospital swiftly after. None of the injuries she sustained were serious. However, during the stay at the hospital, the doctors discovered that she had some form of cardiac arrhythmia. They recommended installing a pacemaker to get her heart back up to speed. The operation went by without a hitch, although minor complications thereafter resulted in her stay at the hospital being extended. She was in the hospital for weeks. I tried to imagine what she did, thought, or felt outside of visiting hours, the days measured by visits and recovery milestones.

I wondered too how my grandfather's everyday must have been given a different contour because of the event. In recent years, he had become a Beckettian character. He rarely came out of his flat, repeated the stories he had told before, and loved eating bananas. He seemed to be lodged in the past, in an inflation-less, pre-globalisation reality. He found common things absurdly expensive and continued to believe in the sanctity of office hours. Given his hermetic lifestyle, he had become excluded from our common time and struggled to re-connect to this differing perception of reality. He inhabited a certain world between the now, memory, and imagination, without a conventional understanding of time and place.

One day, I too will fall out of sync with this common time. I often speculate about how it will happen. I think of promises and disasters, the first an illusive way of connecting to this collective time, and the latter a disruption, existing outside, altering our common mode of meaning. Time, even when it has lost its shape, sweeps us along, sculpts us, scars us, scratches

spoils

[3]

The growths have been there for some time now. I don't remember when it happened, or how it happened. I suppose it must have happened gradually at first—a trickle, and then a flood. They became increasingly unsightly, and I always wondered when they would stop.

They seem to have a purpose, a destiny, as though on their way to expressing some final meaning, as though showing me my body's true and grotesque form.

Worried that these menacing pink bumps could be cancerous growths, I sought an expert opinion and learnt that they were keloids. Keloids are a form of scar tissue, typically developing with no obvious trauma. They are scars that emerge over time. Sometimes, it itches, but I get afraid of scratching at them. Sometimes, it hurts, a pinching pain, but there is nothing I can do about that. And sometimes they don't bother me at all. Over the years, this deformed flesh has blossomed, spreading slowly but surely. Is there is a limit to their influence? Will they find their final definition? I don't know.

I always saw them as something outside of myself. After all, we typically reject things that we consider to be marks of ugliness. I got steroid injections that were supposed to improve their appearance, but I didn't persist with the treatment, and they kept on growing. They didn't belong on my body. I wanted them removed.

The word "keloid" is derived from ancient Greek, meaning "hoof". A part of the body, a part that belongs—just perhaps not a human's.

[4]

At the age of 12, I received a BCG vaccination, as all Singaporean children do. The jab left a red bump on my left arm, which I was told would be permanent. I didn't mind because everyone else would be marked in the same way too. The scar signified a shared experience, and hence it was easier to accept. It expanded my notion of what my body was at an age when it was on the cusp of puberty: my body was not simply a thing that grew on its own, and there were reasons that we would wilfully induce transformation. But the memory of this understanding faded after a while, and when the keloids appeared on my chest, it startled me.

Over time, the bump on my arm has receded, as though it has been absorbed back into my body, and it is now barely visible. I suppose I was lied to. The body shifts in ways unexpected.

[5]

I went back to the doctor's recently, concerned once again that the keloids were something more life-threatening than simple scar tissue. They seemed to have changed after some years. I lifted my shirt and pointed at them to the doctor, who assured me that it was nothing to worry about, and that keloid scars rarely stay the same over time. For the rest of the afternoon, I kept thinking about the keloids, preoccupied with the notion that they were still transforming according to some imperceptible destiny.

[6]

Barely a year old, I embellished myself with a scar on my chin. I had only just learnt to walk. We had just moved to a new flat, and as I excitedly began exploring the new place, I tripped just as I was about to enter the balcony. My chin landed on a small step, drawing blood. I don't remember the incident. The scar is barely visible, so much so that sometimes I doubt it is even there. But it must be. The body remembers what the mind does not.

[7]

When I was 17, I participated in a school band performance at the Singapore Botanic Gardens. I did many senseless things as a child, a habit that I had embarrassingly failed to outgrow even at 17. Hence, when one of my fellow clarinettists wanted to pull a prank on another of our compatriots after the performance, I foolishly agreed. I don't even remember what the prank was. I was supposed to ambush the target somehow. He was supposed to first be startled and then happily surprised. It was a very low standard of prank.

Alas, I slipped as I was about to pounce, falling on my chin. My instrument case burst open, flinging pieces of unassembled clarinet across the path. There was very little pain, but I was mortified. I scrambled to pick up the instrument and made an untidy exit.

When I got home, my father accompanied me to a clinic, the only one in the vicinity open so late in the evening. The doctor didn't say much, and quickly got to the cleaning and the stitches. He wore a mask the entire time I was there, so I could only see his eyes. Keen to hide my shame, I simply looked away at a light fixture and stared into its blankness as the first scar on my chin was overwritten with the new one.

[8]

I have lived here almost all my life and still I struggle to hold onto this space that I inhabit. The playground with the gigantic face that terrified me as a child is gone. New blocks of flats have appeared, obscuring the view. Old bus routes and now-abandoned bus stations are but hazy memories. There are no more snakes or bats, barely any centipedes. Everything is now a different colour.

I spend barely half a year away and I come back to new sky-scrapers and vanished buildings. Old meeting places gone. Lost voices, flavours, sights, sounds.

Life always accelerates. I see it in my father, who has been nostalgic of late. He tries to remember disappeared places in vain. He mentions the National Theatre, now commemorated in a monument, an excerpt of its former glory. He visits the former site of his alma mater and laments that he will never see it again. He describes dating spots and eating places now accessible only through memory and imagination. He knows he is running out of time.

Through his words, I chart a geography of time. I begin to wonder what it's like to see life

at his speed

[9]

Sometimes, at lunchtime, I leave the office and take a walk down to the Padang, the field of grass in front of the former City Hall and Supreme Court buildings, now the National Gallery. The area is home to several war memorials, including the Cenotaph, which remembers both 124 British soldiers—either born in Singapore or residents here—who died in the First World War, and the casualties of the

Second. It has a rating on Google Maps that currently stands at four-point-three out of five. Nearby are the Lim Bo Seng Memorial and the Civilian War Memorial, the latter being comprised of four square pillars and is colloquially known as the "Chopsticks Monument" or "The Chopsticks". As marks of national trauma, such monuments are among the few architectural structures that can resist the tide of urban change.

[10]

In Satoshi Kon's 2001 film *Millennium Actress*, Genya Tachibana drags a cameraman along in the twilight days of the bankrupt Ginei Studios, hoping to complete a documentary on Chiyoko Fujiwara, one of the biggest stars during its golden age. Now elderly and retired, the actress begins to recount to them her storied career. As she speaks, filmic fiction and personal history intermingle, and the line between truth and fiction grows blurred.

Curiously, the interviewers zip in and out of her life story, as history, biography, and fiction are woven into a coherent whole. They become participants, active spectators that enable the reconstruction of the complex experience of time and an impossibly shared history. Nothing separates them from their surrounding reality, a fact realised by the fluid, malleable line of animation.

In animation, the body and the writing become one, mirroring the film's narrative and presentation. Like the films that they so seamlessly blend into, Chiyoko's stories are just moments, projections of experience, fragments of remembrance employed in a performance. These lines that animate her—that animate us—they are engravings, writings, words. They bring a story to life, one that matches the truth of physical reality with the gift of experience. We should not pretend that stories allow us into the world of another, to inhabit another subjectivity. Rather, they are the trace, the mark of an entryway, through which we become the actors, the texts.

[11]
For a long time, all I knew about the Occupation came from museum exhibitions, textbooks, and a local television series called *The Price of Peace*. The exhibitions contained artefacts divorced from their reality. Textbooks focused on the broad strokes, before zooming in and offering heroic accounts of individuals such as Lieutenant Adnan bin Saidi and Elizabeth Choy. In its heavy-handedness, the television series betrayed its fictional texture. My knowledge of the war was a narrative not untrue, and yet, with nothing quite true.

[12]
As a young girl, Chiyoko falls in love with an anti-war revolutionary who also happens to be a painter. It is this that gives us the central image of the film—a fractured vision of Chiyoko on a rickshaw, on a bicycle, on her own feet, sprinting through different movie sets, different eras, her body and clothes transforming. Ostensibly, she is chasing after the man, but in the broader context, she is running to her future—these are her deformations, her traumas, her accomplishments, her dreams.

[13]

Chiyoko stops her search for the man eventually. When asked why years later, she explains that he would no longer be able to recognise her—the painting of her now but an image of lost youth. But there is also the implication that he too would have changed, his body ruined by the violence of war, his mind transformed by the ordeal of the years. There would be nothing of the man that she had fallen in love with left, only mangled flesh.

[14]

My father's memory seems to decline by the day. Perhaps like my grandfather before him, he is losing his ability to stay with the pulse of the world around him.

What terrifies me most is such an arrhythmic existence.

[15]

Grandfather died. It wasn't unexpected, but it still caught us by surprise.

The wake began on a Friday, continued on Saturday, and on Sunday, the funeral took place. It was a Christian funeral, attended primarily by members of the church that my grandparents belonged to.

I told myself that everything has its time, its moment. I supposed that it was true. But then, as I looked through the few photos of my grandfather that I had, I discovered how unprepared we can be for such moments.

My father had never looked older to me, my uncle never more vulnerable. My sister trawled our modest collection of old photographs for images of my grandfather. I didn't do the same. I recognised its value, as comfort and as nostalgia, but I think I was afraid. Within such archaeological work lurks the danger of erasure, that the act of unearthing will force memory into confrontation with evidence, will reveal the past to foreign air and harsh sunlight. Disintegration, dust

barely even a trace

[16]

The last time I saw him alive, he was deep in troubled sleep. He had been in the same bed of the same ward for weeks. I stood there silently on his left, my mother on the other side. His eyes were moving rapidly under his eyelids. Occasionally, his face and arms twitched. His body breathed in a laboured manner. His hands were cold. His false teeth had been removed and set aside in a plastic box next to the bed, changing the shape of his face. It was obvious that he was fast fading.

It felt awkward, as though the last moments of his life had in fact already passed imperceptibly and we were simply awaiting the pronouncement of death. We had been standing silently for minutes when I noticed the tears on my mother's face. I felt almost jealous, as though she had accessed a deep sadness that was unavailable to me. She stepped out of the ward to collect herself. I stayed. I'm not sure why I did. I must have felt an obligation, in the sense that it was the last thing I could do for him—or myself. Underneath the churning of the hospital machinery and the machinery of the human body, there was a heavy silence.

As I stepped away from his bedside, I could hear nothing but the sound of his breathing, as though the space of my mind could admit nothing else. It was irregular and he perpetually sounded like he was on the verge of choking on something. I went to the sink and took off the gloves, the mask, and the disposable gown. I took too long to wash my hands, and as I looked up and into the mirror, I saw that my face looked just like his. My eyes became wet, and it seemed that I too had discovered sorrow.

[17]

He would sometimes tell us about the war, but never in any concrete terms. That is, he would skirt around it and tell us about the smallest excerpts from his life. There was no judgement in my grandfather's tales, no politics, no anger. They tended to be the things that he treasured rather than the things he regretted. He never spoke about how hard it may have been. Perhaps he was still trying to measure the extent of his trauma after all those years.

He worked briefly for a Japanese man as a clerk. When his employer was about to leave Singapore, he wanted to entrust his daughter to my grandfather, but my grandfather was already married by then—he married when he was 19—and so that never came to pass. Once, he had to escape certain danger on a train. Another time, he was asked to do a menial task by an angry Japanese soldier. Thankfully, there was no follow-up. There are so many different turns his life could have taken. Whenever I think about this, my existence seems retrospectively precarious.

He wasn't, by any measure, a great storyteller. The stories always came in fragments, as though he had suddenly thought of something, or he was just skipping to the parts that he liked. There was also a conspicuous void, none of the ugliness of war, no death. I had always supposed that it was implicit in the tales, and that it wasn't what he wanted his grandchildren to inherit. Because of their anecdotal nature and limited scope, they always felt divorced from their original meaning. He repeated them often. Perhaps he wanted to remember it in a specific way, and repetition was a way of establishing a particular reality.

[18]

He was hard of hearing, and conversations always seemed to fall out of sync. Yet, there was something fitting about that, as though it reflected how we were of different rhythms or different speeds. Asynchronous, I was never able to enter the worlds that he had seen.

[19]

At the wake, the hours passed slowly. During a lull in proceedings, I walked out of the hall and wandered. Shortly I found myself in Bidadari Cemetery, where Lim Boon Keng had been buried. Lim was a Peranakan physician who contributed to educational and social reforms in Singapore. For some years, Lim was blamed for becoming party to the Japanese efforts to subdue the local Chinese population, because he took up leadership of the Overseas Chinese Association, an organisation supposedly founded to mediate between the Chinese people in Singapore and the Japanese authorities, but truthfully was a means by which the Japanese extorted millions from the local Chinese. In fact, he almost certainly made the decision to lead the association to protect family members interred at a concentration camp, but he may also have tried to protect other people in that position, slyly disregarding some of his orders, and one time even pretending to be in a drunken stupor to escape his duties.

[20]

My family once sat outdoors at a Starbucks in Clarke Quay after a meal with my grandparents. We could see the Singapore River from where we were sitting. My grandfather had worked for a printing shop here back in the day, and that afternoon, he told us about a man standing in the river. Apparently, desperate that his wife had left him, the man stood in the water threatening to take his own life. But at sunset, the water had risen so much that it frightened him. He started to scream for help. My grandfather laughed as he mentioned this, but I'm sure the gravity of the situation was quite different in the moment.

I have always loved that story. The details are sketchy. And I know I could have listened better, remembered more. We receive so much, we retain so little. And perhaps he could have said more, but there is potency in its ambiguity.

168

[21]

In the eulogy, I wrote about the disconnected things I could remember about my grandfather, about how he could speak so many languages and dialects when I could barely manage one, about how he would high-five me as a way of saying goodbye, about his smile, which is the same smile that I wear, about the sound of his voice. I wrote about how he would often remind me that our family descended from Dabu in Guangdong, as though he'd like to see it—or that he'd like me to see it. I wrote about how he liked to have the entire family together at gatherings, but also liked sitting in a corner, apart from everyone else, watching things unfold, as though he was proud of how this family had come together.

But I also emphasised how there were many things I couldn't say about my grandfather, many things I didn't know, didn't remember. The things I failed to recall, the things he never told us. I realised then that despite this, my body would always carry this memory of him, like one of those stories he would tell, or perhaps does not need telling, a persistent remembrance beyond my own recollection, present

out of reach

[22]

The crowd spoke primarily Cantonese. I didn't want to speak in Cantonese. I didn't want to speak in Mandarin. I wanted to speak in the voice that the thoughts occurred to me. I put my fear of speaking for the dead—of presuming too much of the people who no longer had voices—first and wrote somewhat carefully around the idea that there was so much that was unknowable—that would remain unknowable—to me and to everyone else. I didn't want them to write his story for him. I wanted to avoid telling his tale.

I knew that some things took time, especially how to talk about a death, a loss, a pain beyond words, but the eulogy was required there and then. I wanted to say something in a way that was mine, but instead I only found the vacantness of my words. The void was filled by the onrush of feelings, divorced from actual thoughts or meaning. I was little more than a symbol performing the way the mind loses control of the body.

In the end, it was a fool's errand. In trying to give him as much respect as I could afford, I thought only about myself. In the end, in trying not to speak for him, I spoke for him. In the end, everything comes to the light, decaying, destroyed.

[23]

I think back to the stories of *Millennium Actress*, to the images, to the lines, devoid of substance, and yet full of life. I think of how an experienced truth can outlast its initial occurrence. If everything truly has its time, then it also means that some things continue beyond their material existence. I look in the mirror again and I realise that I am a part of my grandfather's story, something that exists in the beyond, a ghost rendered in flesh. I wear his face, an out-of-sync echo.

In telling the story, embodied by tears, by scar tissue, I continue to play out this personal history. We each are the archive. We each are the scars.

everything has its time in its time

[24]

Time passes through us. The future vanishes, each instant purgatorial, every moment our catastrophe. I catch a glimpse of an enduring meaning, something lasting beyond its boundaries. There is a picture of you, a picture of us, constantly falling out of pace with each other—and ourselves. I embrace this state, negotiating, renegotiating, affirming and disavowing the distances between us. I am an imprint, an impression, a trace in the sand that somehow persists. And your every action deforms my being, leaves an inscription. This body, this memory, this flesh, it is a trace of you. A word, a line, a poem, a song, a scar.

▪ Ghost Stories

2020

One morning, a ghost appeared in the corner of the room. It was damp and green, like a mossy sponge. The ghost was a mound about four feet tall, and on its uneven surface, there were relief configurations that almost looked like a face. I wasn't afraid even though it was like nothing I had ever seen before and it had no reason to be there. In fact, there was a certain calmness about its presence, as though it had always belonged in the room, in that corner, as though it was finally ready to make its presence known to me.

I wasn't sure what to do about it. To be frank, I had spent my entire life being sceptical of the paranormal—specifically when it came to the

▌ The entry is near the end of the notebook, I think. There is even a sketch of the page, and something written down, something incorporating the words "mossy and green".

▌ The idea first occurred to me about ten years ago. Maybe it wasn't so much an idea as it was an image. At the time, I had read a book by César Aira titled existence of ghosts. But I had also spent my entire life being a coward. Horror movies were always able to make me jump even if I didn't believe in ghosts.

At first, this unexpected turn of events left me unsure of what to do. I wasn't even certain that I could believe my eyes. Reality takes time to settle down—to properly percolate— immediately after one wakes up. So I waited for five minutes and looked again—but the ghost remained. I stayed in the bed for a long time, not because I was afraid, but because nothing in my admittedly shallow life experience could tell me

Ghosts. It was my introduction to the writer, and it left a deep impression, but I suppose I have always been fascinated by the paranormal in the first place.

I didn't touch the idea for a long time after that. Not long after I had put it down on paper, I retired the notebook. Sandwiched between two other notebooks, the ghost sat waiting for its moment for years.

❙ In the first half of the 2010s, I became obsessed with writing stories about characters suffering from some great disquiet, typically some kind of unnamed illness—an inexplicable nausea, a third eye sprouting, a left-right reversal in perception, an inability to see any human faces—perhaps reflecting my own discomfort with my own body. Over time, it became more and more of a crutch that I would lean on just to give the what to do. I stayed still and observed for what must have been a quarter of an hour. It was certainly alive though it made almost no sound.

Eventually, I climbed out of bed and approached it gingerly, for fear of frightening it. It was only when I drew nearer that I could see the crags and pore across its surface. It didn't seem to be breathing, but can the human eye really observe a sponge or a starfish breathing?

I thought of calling up my friend to let her know that there was a ghost in the room. It was her place, after all, and as temporary caretaker, it was my responsibility to let her know about such unexpected developments. But I hesitated. There was a harmlessness— no, helplessness—to the ghost that gave pause. I didn't want to snitch on the ghost. I didn't

story a bit of strangeness.

In retrospect, I wonder if the ghost idea took root in a type of opposition to this internal phenomenological drama. As I grew older, I grew tired of the existential questions of my teens and became more invested in the idea of connection.

❚ I still haven't taken out the notebook. There is a sense that it might not live up to its promise. The impression in my mind has become its own reality, and I fear that looking at the page would dismantle it.

want to be the bad guy. Maybe it would be gone the next day.

My friend had asked me to look after her place for six months while she was away. She was an academic from Sichuan who had to take on a project back home, and because there was no way she could suspend her rental agreement, it was just more efficient for her to put someone else in the guest room to take care of the miscellaneous chores and not let the rent go to waste. As a writer working freelance jobs just to put Gardenia bread on the table, I accepted the offer to have a place to myself for six months, so that I could complete a novel about a conman falling out of pace with modern times that had been derailed by my freelance work. That is, I thought of it as kind of a friendship writing residency.

❚ I quickly realised that for this story to succeed, the protagonist had to live by himself. It became a play of distances and separations. Or rather, it became about the connections that persist despite distances and separations.

When I wrote the story, much like with the choice of the ghost as plot device, I opted for something inauthentic and hard to believe, yet somehow it seemed truer to the internal tenor of that which was and is experienced.

The guestroom featured a desk, power sockets galore, a simple bed, Wi-Fi, and some decorations. I was also allowed to use the kitchen so long as I kept it clean. My duties included watering the plants, checking the mail, collecting parcels, and the occasional light cleaning. And of course, I was to take care of any water and electricity bills that came.

We first met as university classmates several years ago, when I still aspired to become a scientist. She said that she had taken up a government scholarship and had come from Zigong. At the time, I knew nothing about Zigong, and the only thing that she told me was that many dinosaurs came from Zigong. I had always had a fondness for dinosaurs, and I guess that's why, even though we had almost nothing

❙ I did indeed have a classmate in university from Zigong. We were never really close at all, but it was convenient soil on which to plant this fictional friendship. What she had said was 自貢出恐龍 (*Zigong chu konglong*), a catchy rhyme of a sort that just means that dinosaurs come from Zigong.

in common, we became fast friends. When she mentioned it, I started rambling on and on about fossils and why they were so fascinating to me. I haven't mentioned this yet, but I'm kind of socially inept.

Fossils had always fascinated me because they felt like objects from a different reality, things that had time travelled. The joint was out of its time, so to speak. Emerging again millions of years after their initial formation, they had all effectively shed their immediate substance to become symbols, texts, to be interpreted in a language invented millions of years after the instance of death. That is, despite their very material existence— bones, amber, petrified wood, oil, DNA—there was nothing left of the body, no breathing, circulation, digestion. Just texts,

❚ I had been obsessed with dinosaurs from a young age, which I attribute to a boxed set of Isaac Asimov board books, each explaining in simple detail the life of a particular dinosaur. Some of this new knowledge would later be updated as the science of dinosaurs continued to evolve. What I had yet to grasp at that time, however, that the storytelling mattered far more than the facts.

I collected books about dinosaurs, the largest of which was—and probably still is— larger than my face. Though I can't claim to have read all of them from cover to cover, words, signs. Like semiotic ghosts of a sort.

I remember spending many afternoons flipping through them. I wasn't learning much, but there was a visceral joy in doing so, perhaps because those books inhabited the intersection between science education and fantastical thrill.

It was also around that time that *Jurassic Park* first hit the theatres. As you can imagine, I was in love with the film. I've never read the book. I was ecstatic when my aunt promised to take me to the cinema to catch *The Lost World*, and oddly, I remember that emotion better than I remember the film.

Conceptually, the premise of *Jurassic Park* is a form of time travel. Many time travel plots have to do with a type of disruption, characters displaced in time—the classic fish out of water scenario. Typically, this is played for humour, but in this sense, *Jurassic Park* is more like *The Terminator*, with time travellers that are monstrous to humans.

Yet, on the part of the dinosaurs—genetic revenants from a world devoid of humankind, human technology, human culture—they are thrust into an encounter with a species capable of greatest cruelty. *Jurassic Park* is fantasy, and in that sense, it is something that captures the impossible. It depicts our arrogance, our wilful unkindness, and our desire to disrupt time as cinematic spectacle.

I decided to call my grandmother instead. She was sure to have an answer. She was the only family I had, and we lived in a small flat in Toa Payoh. In

❙ My grandmother passed away in 2019. Initially, I wanted desperately to write about her and her death in an essay, but that proved to be a pointless

order to ensure that I made the most of this time I set aside for myself, I tried not to go home too much. I wanted to adhere to a strict regimen over this time to ensure that I would concentrate on my writing. I wanted it to feel different from my usual routine. Grandma was fairly independent despite her age, which helped me to take up this temporary isolation scheme.

exercise. It felt hollow, the rote repetition of familiar motions, writing without spirit or substance. Perhaps because it came so soon after the deaths of my aunt and my grandfather, another wave in that proverbial sea of sorrow.

I became too aware that something factually true could still come off as inauthentic, as lies. But then, the image of the mossy ghost surfaced again shortly after the funeral was over, and I started to experiment with it as a story. I wrote in a hurry, keen to capture the feeling of it before the moment passed, before it became just pure memory. Only when I had finished did I realise that the opposite occurred. A tale utterly absurd and clearly fabricated could ring truer than any reportage. Thus I recognised the path of fiction as

Grandma spoke primarily Cantonese, but she always spoke to me in Mandarin because, when I was growing up, she believed that it would help me in school. An approximate translation of our exchange:

Grandma, I saw a—

Have you eaten?

I'm fine. I saw— I mean, how about you?

I've just had lunch.

That's great. Uh, Grandma, I uh—

Yes?

I think I saw a ghost, Grandma.

What?

Yeah, it's short, and dirty green, and kind of—

A ghost?

the path of disruption.

❙ This is probably not true. In real life, she spoke in Mandarin to the grandchildren because the grandchildren never picked up Cantonese, at least not until we were older, by which time the basis of linguistic exchange had already solidified. I don't really think my grandmother worried that much about how we were doing in school.

❙ When we were much younger, my sister would ring up my grandparents and engage in conversation that was never particularly meaningful. Rather, it was a form of banter, a form of play. I didn't do any of this, partly because I was about half her age at the time that this was occurring. I also kept to myself more, and was always bad at speaking or conversations in the first place, and so, would always feel stressed at the idea that I

Kind of damp. It doesn't really have a face but—I just know it's a ghost.

She didn't say a word.

It just appeared in the corner of the room. It's still sitting there.

There was a long, long silence. It was at about that point that I realised I was never really going to get through to her. Certainly, people of her generation were likely to have a greater appreciation

had to chat with my elders—and over the phone too, where quiet moments were not filled with expressions or actions or any tangible distraction but electronic silence.

This conversation would never have happened, not this way, because I never called, and more broadly speaking, I was hardly as close to her as the story sets up its two major characters. Yet, call it convenient shorthand, or deception, or a form of cheating, but there remains something true about it, a certain sentimental attachment, a certain bond that did not present itself so visibly.

❚ It's not to say that the older generation are more superstitious, but perhaps there has always been the impression that they were more in tune with the spiritual than the younger ones, who had been tainted by of the spiritual or indeed the paranormal, but my grandmother was also a devout Christian, and so she was never really into the whole ghosts and ghouls thing. I don't really think anyone can deduce all that much from a silence across a phone line, but it didn't seem like she was mad or panicking. She was probably just trying to figure out a reasonable explanation for my behaviour.

Never mind, I said. It'll probably be gone tomorrow.

cynicism and capitalism.

❙ Around the time that I entered university, I started to read much more translated modern and contemporary literature. I was first drawn to the Latin American writers, from the Boom writers to Roberto Bolaño, but soon found my way to different parts of the world. As my interest in reading translated literature from different cultures and places around the globe burgeoned, my interest in the work of translation grew as well. Yet, as much as I seemed, on the surface, well-equipped to tackle this challenge—I was not—it intimidated me, and there was a misguided sense that my floundering attempts would be disrespectful to the original texts and their authors.

My interest in translation persisted and although it soon became part of my day job, I produced texts that were functional more than anything else. One day, I naively decided to start trying my hand at literary translation. I chose a short story by a Chinese writer and dived in headfirst. All I emerged with, however, was a very sterile end-product. In the end, what disappointed me was less the inability to successfully render meaning as accurately as I had first aspired to, but the

184

She didn't refer to it again for the rest of the phone call, and I chipped in too, doing my best to pretend that everything was okay, and that I hadn't really called her to talk about Casper the Friendly Ghost. We talked for another 15 minutes, and through it all, I didn't look away from the ghost. It was almost imperceptible, but there was a change in its demeanour, as though it was comforted by the sound of a human voice.

It wasn't gone the next day, so I accepted the fact that I was staying in a haunted house.

You might wonder how

lack of a voice. In effect, it was a machine translation.

▌I wanted the ghost to be unreadable, insofar as it did not use the tools of human communication. And yet, contradictorily, I knew that it had to be possible to understand the ghost, no, to ensure that it would be possible to empathise with it. I wanted it to have human definition even if it didn't have human shape.

I also wanted it so that it would be impossible to infer anything about its life before. That is, I wanted the ghost to be freed from the burden of identity. I wanted it to be human in signification, but without the baggage of biography.

▌For a time, I stopped writing

I knew it was a ghost at first sight. After all, it could have been any manner of strange creature. Was it glowing? Did it send me visions of its former life? Were there tell-tale signs of ectoplasm? I can only say that, no, there was no objective indicator that it was a ghost, but there are some things that you just know. Also, my friend had told me that someone had died in her flat once.

That afternoon, I decided that I would take care of the ghost—which isn't to say that I was going to have it exterminated, but that I would look after its needs. I felt a kind of obligation. On a logical level, I never quite understood the fear of ghosts that people often claimed to have anyway. Certainly, much of it comes out of a fear of the unknown that characterises the afterlife, fiction because I found myself in a creative rut. It felt laborious, rote. It felt like I was going through the same motions over and over, and that repetition or repetitiveness—that ghostly existence—horrified me.

❚ The fear of ghosts is something I've long struggled to understand. Ghosts begin life as humans, and so it has always seemed grossly unfair to me to characterise them as malicious by default.

186

but most ghost stories also preferred malicious renditions, which always disturbed me. After all, weren't human ghosts once human beings too? It seemed unfair to assume that they were all malevolent by default.

For the first five days, the ghost didn't do anything. Every so often, it appeared to drift a little to the left or right, but this appeared to be its natural pulse, and its average position never changed as far as I could tell.

❚ I'm thankful that I work primarily with words and not, say, images. I certainly struggled with imagining how the ghost would move about. If it moved too much, it would become cartoonish. If it didn't move, it would lose its humanity, or worse, become furniture. I targeted a type of uncanny presentation, clearly not human, and yet with echoes enough that it would be unnerving.

When I was a child, there was a popular series of Hong Kong movies involving a giant fungus that had come to life. It

It didn't need to eat. (I checked.) Or drink. (I checked too.)

The ghost had a voice. Sometimes, it would be a whimper like the slow release of air from a balloon. Sometimes it would be a wheeze, not unlike a leaky whistle. And sometimes, it would be a humming, not like a refrigerator or a computer, but like a very old person who didn't realise that they were doing it. Most of the time, however, it was silent, and even at its loudest, it was never enough to cause me any disturbance.

was supposed to be a children's movie, but I remember being quite spooked by it. Now that I think of it, perhaps this ghost was inspired by it.

❚ As this ghost was physical, bodily, and not a spectral image, one had to check.

❚ Looking back, the choice of the ghost's form was a subversion of the stereotypical spectre. These noises could arguably be contrasted against cries of vengeance or great sorrow. More than that, however, it is very bodily, very mechanical.

I imagined the ghost as a physical entity with physical properties: temperature, texture, elasticity. I did not want it to be spectral—that is, an immaterial image or intangible energy. The quickest way to convey this was to borrow from familiar analogues, like, in this

188

case, a balloon.

Similarly, the sounds that it made the mechanical nature of life support, and by extension, life itself. The ghost's wheezing, whimpering, and whistling were allusions to the biological machinery of life.

❚ I've never been much of a believer in the paranormal. The closest I've ever been to one such experience was when I was a member of the school band. I must have been 13 or 14. I played the clarinet, although such a description may be bordering on generous. After a performance one evening, we came back together on a bus to school quite late in the night.

The school sat atop a hill, one face of which had been levelled for the assembly terraces, a massive sports field, and a running track. There were hardly any lights and the bus

On the sixth day, it showed off a new trick. Every so often, the ghost—as if it really was the sponge that it resembled—would release a colourless, odourless liquid onto the vinyl floor. This happened irregularly and silently, but I liked to think that the ghost was embarrassed about it, so I mopped up the fluid on the ground each time. I'm sure I must have imagined it but each time I glanced at the terrestrial feature that I supposed was its face, there seemed to be a look of appreciation.

Other than that, nothing

else of significance happened. This continued for weeks. I got used to its presence, and perhaps it got used to mine. No, it wasn't just a matter of presence, but the individual rhythms of our existence, the things we did in a day, our moods, our tempers. It crossed my mind again to report this incident to my friend, but by then the ghost and I were so well-acquainted that it felt like a betrayal. Besides, my friend had said that it was suicide, that some twenty years ago someone took their own life in this house. That only made me even more sympathetic.

travelled gingerly up the sloping curves towards the peak, where there was a statue and a small clocktower.

As I got off the bus, one of my fellow school band members pointed downwards to the track, which was blanketed in darkness. He said he saw someone there. We gathered around and squinted. There shouldn't have been anyone, certainly not at half past ten in the night, but there it was, a figure, flitting in and out of the darkness. It bobbed up and down, as if exercising, or briskly walking, or marching. We stood transfixed. If it was indeed a person, then the figure was travelling inhumanly quickly.

The teacher acknowledged it briefly. She shushed some of the students who mentioned that there were stories about World War II, suggesting that it could have been a casualty. There was a sense that it was pantang, that we would incur some kind of curse if we spoke too carelessly about it, and so she hurried us along, ushering us towards the band room, where we were to keep our instruments.

As far as I know, none of us ever spoke of the incident again. We simply went home quickly after that, silently agreeing to return this secret to the night.

I went out and took a few books out from the public library, all of which were ghost stories of some sort. I thought that they might help me understand my situation somehow, and in turn, help my writing. Sure, that makes almost no sense, but then again, neither did my situation.

❚ I was an incredibly timid child, and I remember this book with a human skull on the cover with a black background and bloodshot eyes. These days, I laugh when I look back at it, because skulls generally don't come with eyeballs attached. However, the book taught me an important lesson. Despite being

There was some *Mad Max* weather outside, so I came home quickly and spent my afternoon reading. I especially enjoyed the books collecting Japanese kaidan as the spirits in them clearly represented living aspects of the world, while their ghosts tended to have believable, sympathetic motives.

Surveying the different portrayals of our ethereal friends, I came to realise that the concept of ghosts always elicited sympathy for me. You see, ghosts are stuck in time. They are a way that memories manifest. They cannot leave their moment. They don't perform the daily rituals that mark the passing of our days— eating, shitting, sleeping. They don't change their clothes. They don't age. Most ghosts haunt not a place, but a moment— or more accurately, a memory,

terrified of the skull and some of the interior illustrations, I always wanted to read more and more of it. Even as I lost my fear of the unexplained as I grew up, it continued to fascinate me.

❚ *What is a specter made of? Of signs, or more precisely of signatures, that is to say, those signs, ciphers, or monograms that are etched onto things by time.*[1]

Agamben

a story, a trauma. They cannot abandon this station, and hence cannot create anything new. There is nothing left for them, nothing ahead, except deep unrest.

So, being empty, ghosts are little more than photographs or scars, stories that tell themselves, essentially memories. In that, I suppose we all become ghosts, sooner or later.

I Perhaps this repetition is the most frightening, this shrinking of one's existence to a looping phenomenon, unable to regret, unable to learn, void of transformation and connection, little more than luminous shadows. That is, ghosts represent a barrier to knowledge, experience, and change—an agonising coda to life.

I called Grandma again. Initially, I was ready to pester her about this ghost again, thinking that my insistence would eventually win her over. However, this determination dissolved the moment I heard her voice, which was tired, gentle, and

I Recently, I looked at some photos of my grandmother from across a period of decades and it fascinated me how I could only really remember her as she had been in the last few years of her life. Certainly, I could still recognise her in the photos of familiar. She didn't say much except to ask: Are you sure you're taking care of yourself? I thought of the number of times I had lied to her when she'd ask the same question before. I didn't say a thing, but she must have heard me sigh. Suddenly, this whole writing business seemed ridiculous, as though I had abandoned the only family I had left in the world for a childish fantasy. I thought of her face, pale and wrinkled and sagging, smiling and radiant and genial. As if one could really make up for lost time, I said:

I'm coming over later. Around dinnertime.

I'll prepare dinner, she said, her voice brightening.

I took my time, going to get a few of the ang ku kueh that she liked before visiting my favourite café. I had downed two coffees by the time I set

her when she was younger, when my sister was still a toddler, when my dad still had his hair, but there would always be an intervening step, a momentary uncertainty, the extra effort needed to confirm that it was her. It was as though that image of her in the final few years of her life had become so well-defined to me that it had essentially overwritten everything else that had come before, fossil, frozen.

❙ Every literary text is laced with regret, which may be invisible to the reader—and sometimes even the author.

❙ Most of my writing is a patchwork of half-truths and convenient fictions. Sometimes this is brought on by practical need, filling in the gaps that off for home. When I arrived, Grandma was standing at the small electric stovetop that she did all her cooking on these days. In the pot was her version of the Foochow dish red vinasse chicken. I once asked her if she could teach me how to cook it, but she refused. Maybe she wanted to keep her secrets, or maybe she thought that a guy should stay out of the kitchen— she could be traditional in that sort of way. Or maybe it was an insurance policy, to keep me by her side.

I can't otherwise, or giving coherence to the fragments available to me. In some other cases, this is deliberate—wilful, even. Facts serve as confirmation, but fiction can come closer to the true texture of experience.

I put down my stuff in my room, then asked her if I could help. She just shooed me away. So I took a look around the house. It felt as if time had been dilated, or maybe intensified. I hadn't been away for that long, and yet it felt like years.

I looked inside her room

❙ We had never lived in the same house before, and perhaps this is partly why I needed to artificially manufacture the frankly absurd premise that the protagonist had moved out for a while.

a gap, an absence in my experience

writing from the outside.

❙ I kept certain details about

to see that everything was in its place. To one side of the room was the bed that belonged to Grandpa. He left us last year at the age of 93. For months they had been keeping an eye on a growth in his gut, certain that it would develop into a full-blown cancer, but in the end, it was a bout of pneumonia that claimed him. He spent his last weeks in the hospital, bedridden. At first, his condition was optimistic, but when he started to weaken, it happened rapidly, and before I knew it, he was on a mechanical respirator and couldn't even open his eyes.

The morning he left, we went to the hospital as soon as we got the phone call. Grandma didn't leave the car. She just stayed in the back of the taxi and cried silently. I can't remember what I said and who I met, but I remember

the place true to life, because it was necessary for me for it to be authentic—it would lose some of its meaning as memorial otherwise. That said, it was also necessary for me that it be a real thing, the way an actor may conceivably find it easier to draw upon personal experience to inform the performance. These details are authentic only to me—they lend nothing to the reader—but they are crucial to the performance. Writing is nothing if not performance.

❚ I remember the afternoon we went to collect him. It was during the weekend, and I remember my mother delivered the news to me when I had just woken up. We took a cab out as soon as we could. Several members of the family went seeing them cart him out on the gurney, covered in a white sheet. From there, the funerary services took over, and I just went along with whatever they suggested was best. The funeral was relatively quiet, all things considered. Grandpa never had many friends. He liked to keep to himself. Besides, he always said to me: Being my age is like missing the bus that most of your friends have got on and having to wait for the next one.

down too to wait for him to be released by the hospital. The sun was punishing that afternoon— unusually bright too, painting the city in an intense chiaroscuro. My grandmother arrived in a car with my uncle's family. She did not step out of it at all, keeping her gaze fixed forwards. I tried to say something to her, but I knew that there was nothing to say. She struggled to keep her tears in. She didn't look at me. She didn't want to look at anyone. Shortly after my grandfather was taken by the funerary services, my uncle drove off.

I remember being at a loss of what to do. My father was visibly shaken. My uncle looked like he was struggling to keep it together. I still wonder if I should have stayed by her side more, but all I have are glimpses.

After the funeral, we cleaned up the bed, but left it

❚ The truth is more mundane. After my grandfather's death, the made, as if we were keeping the light on and expecting him to come home someday.

We had dinner at our small dining table, now made a little larger by Grandpa's absence. Grandma still kept a stool at the side that he used to sit. It may be a cliché to say so, but it was as though he had never really left. I spent the whole evening this way, distracted, and as my thoughts drifted, I looked up at the framed wedding photograph on the circuit breaker next to the main door, secured with a piece of raffia string. In that monochromatic picture, painted in shades that approximated breakfast tea, Grandpa and Grandma were garbed in Western wedding outfits, faces solemn. She was 16 at the time,

bed became superfluous, but it still had practical value. We just struggled to find new owners. Eventually, though it took a long while, it was donated to some neighbours.

❙ Spaces expand and contract when translated into language. Still, I wanted somehow to memorialise the house that they last lived in. Items, artefacts, testifying to its previous life, but also tones, feelings, colours.

❙ The house has, of course, since been sold.

and he was 18.

I had always wanted to ask her what it was like, what was going through her mind. Their marriage had been arranged by the parents, and they barely knew each other when the picture was taken. I wanted to ask if she was happy that day, but I wasn't sure that she would be able to remember a happiness from 75 or 80 years ago. And besides, with time, all memories distort and solidify, abandoning their original substance.

So I kept my thoughts to myself. We ate in a type of peaceful quiet, the way we always did, and I went off shortly after the 10pm news.

The next day, I found myself unable to work. Something had come over me, and it disturbed me that I couldn't

❚ Because I was never as close to them as I would have liked, I always suspected it would have been awkward. There is no real regret, only an acceptance of loss.

quite figure out what it was. I put on music, I made a nice breakfast, I played a video game, but I felt uncomfortable, like a deep unrest had become dislodged and was beginning to metastasise within me.

I found momentary relief in chatting with my roommate. I sat down beside the ghost and told it about my life. I asked it what it was like to die, knowing full well that I would receive no answer. I told it that I didn't miss my parents all that much because the accident happened just before my fourth birthday and I never really got to know them. As a child, I loved those old-fashioned mango birthday cakes, I said.

I talked about Zigong and dinosaurs, and how my favourite dinosaur—the *Dimetrodon*—wasn't a dinosaur at all. I had a plastic toy of a *Dimetrodon*

❚ *methisthanai*: to remove, to change

❚ Fortunately for me, this is mostly fabrication. It is a violent gesture, designed to draw an exceedingly small cast of characters into focus. I felt I was forced to take such dramatic action by the short story form due to my ineptitude, just so I could apprehend the greater feeling of isolation.

I did love those mango birthday cakes, though.

❚ The plastic *Dimetrodon* exists. It sits in a bookcase, a curious congruence between plastic and fossil, one a survivor of deep time, the other a synthetic that could open its jaws if you pushed a button on the tail, and I used to make it chomp on my earlobes. I said to the ghost that I still have the toy today.

I asked if it knew my friend, and said that if it didn't, it would love her. She was the kindest person I knew. I mentioned that one time we were having dinner at a Korean restaurant and I had never seen edamame before in my life, and so I ate the whole fibrous thing, pod and all. She must have noticed my poorly concealed and unusually aggressive chewing, but she never said a single word.

Through all my whining, the ghost kept quiet. It exuded a serenity that calmed me down as well. I wasn't sure that it understood anything that I said, but by the time I stopped, I realised that I had missed my

creation that cannot die, both materials that exist well beyond their moment, ghost and zombie.

❚ This is a concession. Most ghost stories are built on concessions. What we want, in the end, is to engage with the dead, but to do so requires that they speak beyond their moment—to do so demands that our story enters dinner. I apologised for taking up its time and told it that I was going to get a shower and then head to bed.

The night rolled on. Red clouds had unfurled across the sky. Thunder rumbled. The wind was rising. I got up to close the windows but paused for a second— I loved the smell of rain.

I rang Grandma and she sounded as though she was crying. What's wrong? I asked. There was no answer. I'm coming over now, I said, but she assured me that it was fine. She said that all my recent talk about ghosts made her dig up some photos, and there she

a narrative space forbidden to it, and that we too cross over to a narrative space forbidden to us, a transgressive crossing of borders, a narratological act of translation.

❙ Evenings that I treasure, non-specific memories, a pleasure in the repetitive, returning time and again, the redness of clouds, the oncoming rain, streets doused in saffron lights. A personal geography, a secret time, specific, yet repeated. Returning time and again. Returning,

revenant.

saw her son and his wife. It's as though they're still here, she said. But no one is ever really gone. She went onto explain that what made her cry was the realisation that they never got to know me, as though it was me who had been taken from them.

We continued talking about the people who had left us. We didn't say anything that was especially revelatory, and neither of us learnt anything new. In fact, we had talked about these things before. But there was something about that conversation that was different, as though some invisible switch had been flipped, some unseen line crossed.

With the rain battering on the windows and the ghost watching silently from its corner, I slept soundly that night.

| The sound of the rain is a most comforting thing to me in the dead of night. In the story, this represented a shift for me, that the protagonist had grown

so used to the presence of the ghost that he found comfort in it watching over him.

And then, Grandma had a stroke.

I was four months into the stay at my friend's place when it occurred. Things happened very quickly. There was the Incident, and then the Hospitalisation, and then the Deterioration, and then the Silence, and then the Funeral, all within the span of three weeks. There were many people who came to see her off. She had been a very active and well-loved member of her congregation at church. Everyone expressed their sadness, but it all annoyed me because our grief was not the same. That is, they could never know the grandmother who raised me, the grandmother I lived with, the grandmother who faced her sadness with dignity. They just knew the woman who was devout and kind.

I was too shaken to handle the eulogy. Fortunately, one of the church leaders was said to be like a son to her and he was happy to take on the task. I just spent as much time as I could sitting in a corner by myself, away from the crowds, away from the voices. I didn't want to talk. However, some relatives from Malaysia that I didn't recognise came to greet me and offer their sympathies. I tried to keep myself from breaking down. One of them, a distant cousin, handed me a photograph of Grandma. She said that they had found it at home before coming down. I

❘ In reality, I had to handle the eulogy. I was extremely reluctant to. Apart from feeling as though there were people better positioned to talk about her, it was impossible to explain the Derridian fear of speaking for others, who can no longer speak for themselves. I was deeply uncomfortable with the idea. I saw no way I could escape my own voice. In truth, every eulogy is selfish, because the message is for ourselves, because the other is the story that we tell ourselves, the memory that we must reckon with.

I did the eulogies for both my grandfather and

thanked her.

In the photo, Grandma looked like she was in her fifties. She wore tinted glasses and a white hat. My teenage father stood next to her. Something about it disturbed me and, not wanting to have to deal with it then, I slotted the photo into my diary.

On the third day of proceedings, I watched as her remains were sent into the incinerator on a motor-driven

grandmother. Both texts still feel grotesque. They were oppositional to what I believed I should have said. What I wanted was to present silence. In the aftermath of loss, the wordlessness was crushing. Instead, I wrote vaguely subversive pieces that tried to foreground the impossibility of knowing someone else, yet still mired in the too-familiar rhetoric of grief.

❚ There's no such photo. At least, I don't think there is. I'm no longer sure if it is a memory or a figment of my imagination.

cart. Around me, there was a lot of weeping. One of the men from the church had brought a guitar into the observation area, and midway through proceedings, he roused the weeping crowd into a Mandarin rendition of "Amazing Grace". The loudness of the chorus felt at odds with what was happening, but I didn't mind. I think Grandma would have appreciated it. She would sometimes put on hymns on the old cassette player if she had trouble sleeping.

And then, after the song, after the funeral, there was just unbearable silence.

For the next week, I didn't leave the house. I barely even left the room. I couldn't bring myself to. There were a lot of tears, and also fear—inexplicable fear, overbearing, awful. I was scared to even go to the bathroom.

❚ This actually happened at my grandfather's funeral. I think it was the man who often led Sunday School when I was a child. In fact, it was quiet when my grandmother's remains were delivered into the incinerator. There were a lot of tears. There was no singing.

❚ A friend of mine, Z, read the story and started pointing out to me parts of my life that he recognised. Z tends to do that, claiming to spot these supposedly biographical bits, and then reading into it some

The world trembled every time I stepped out of the bed. I kept the lights off at all times. I slept very little. I ate even less. I ignored my need for food for as long as I could, and almost convinced myself not to buy any groceries. But I knew it wasn't what Grandma would have wanted, so I just ordered them online and someone left them outside the door.

I thought about returning home, instead of staying at my friend's, but I wasn't ready to face the space that she used to inhabit. Besides, at least I wasn't alone here. Through it all, the ghost was a silent witness, giving me the space to grieve, indulging my unexplainable fear of the world.

understanding. I think it is reassuring to him. It gives him the illusion of knowledge. I usually play along, although the finality of these casual proclamations sometimes grates, and I think, perhaps he has yet to uncover the relationship between authenticity and fabrication, between picture and performance.

❚ Every text begins life with an uncertain shape, shambling, and is sculpted into a clearer definition, until it meets a final shape. Thus pronounced, it reaches its death

no

such a view disregards the performance of text, its growth, its metamorphoses. We must strive to resist the tyranny of finality, of death. I know that these right-sided texts must seem like interruptions, like annotations, or worse, hiccups. Unlike the story to the left, they lack a certain coherence, lack unity. But these are not intervention. They are not insertions, interruptions, addenda. They are a way for me to return to texts past, or perhaps more accurately, they are a way for me to revive dead moments, summoning them, bringing time out of joint.

One night, I looked at that photo of Grandma with the aid of the glow from my phone. It felt brittle in my hand. I noticed how different her smile was back then. Then I put it down. Something about it provoked a violent reaction in me. I felt sick.

| Revenant,
from *revenir*,
to return

Suddenly it occurred to me that I hadn't said a single word in a whole week. So, as scared as I was, I crawled out of the sheets, photograph in

| The image has the ability to haunt, and despite the often multisensorial nature of their materialisation—sound, temperature, kinetic evidence—

hand, and sidled up next to the ghost. Leaning back against the wall, I sat on the floor, staring at it. Minutes passed. It almost seemed to be waiting patiently for me. When I could finally summon the words, I said, my voice cracking: Another one. I'm all alone now.

The tears were relentless. With great effort, I placed the photo on the floor, right next to the ghost. I didn't want to touch it again. She was gone, I thought. Gone. And the photograph was a grotesque reminder of my new reality.

ghosts are still essentially image.

Suddenly I saw Pascale's face, which I knew was a dead woman's face, come onto the screen. She answered my question: "Do you believe in ghosts?" Practically looking me in the eye, she said to me again, on the big screen: "Yes, now I do, yes." Which now? Years later in Texas, I had the unnerving sense of the return of her specter, the specter of her specter coming back to say to me—to me here, now: "Now... now... now, that is to say, in this dark room on another continent, in another world, here, now, yes, believe me,

210

I believe in ghosts."[2]

Derrida

I limped back to bed and cried until I could fall asleep.

I woke with a start in the middle of the night. Next to me on the bed, bent over and staring at me in the darkness, was the ghost. We looked at each other for moments. It felt like our eyes met even though it didn't have any. Then it made a noise I had never heard it make before, a soft humming, like a mother hushing her child to sleep. And then it moved. I couldn't see it clearly in the dark and without my glasses, but it almost looked like it had a hand, and it was holding something.

It placed the object on my chest. By the time I found my glasses, it had turned its back towards me and was shuffling

▌ A ghost is an absence, a lack,

a wound on our being

▌ Every text is a ghost, an unchanging signifier, a permanent configuration to which we return time again, and away. The object was the photograph of Grandma. After weeks and weeks of a type of grossly limited communication, this was its first real message to me. And as I looked at the photograph, familiar words echoed in my mind: No one is ever really gone.

I held onto the photograph and looked up at the ghost again. Sluggishly, it retreated to its corner, and then, as if it had finally said what it had waited months to say, it slowly dissolved into the darkness. It never returned.

which returns to us time and again. In each text that we read, we watch, we write, we sing, we see traces of ourselves from other days, fossils, time travellers, spectres of forbidden domains.

❚ Stay, he said. Stay, illusion.

❚ The photographs hide so much more, so many stories that she knew, she experienced, but all I have is the surface, the spectre, no embodiment, just memory, just image.
❚ Every story is a ghost story. Each remembrance, each image,

each anecdote is a material-
isation of another, the other,
in our lives. Inscribed in our
memory, summoned by our
acts of reading, limited by our
retellings. Every story is a ghost
story, every story is a ghost.

■ Metamorphoses (II)

2017

perhaps cinders perhaps sound

In *Strange Tales from a Chinese Studio*, Pu Songling tells the tale of a beggar-monk who spends his days reciting the sutras on the streets and begging for alms. He rejects all offers of food and drink, and is never seen eating anything. One day, a person suggests to him to try the countryside. The term used for the begging of alms here is 化緣 (*huayuan*), a Buddhist term that implies choosing to accumulate good karma, and more literally means to transform one's fate. The beggar-monk protests and claims, This is exactly how I am seeking to transform!

Sometime later, the beggar-monk lies motionless on the side of the road. He remains in this position for three days. Afraid of him starving to death, passersby offer him food and money, which he rejects with silence, eyes shut. The crowd grows concerned, begins gesticulating, shouting, shaking him. In a fit of rage, the beggar-monk opens his eyes, draws a knife from his robe, and disembowels himself.

The people are terrified and notify the authorities, who arrive far too late. All they manage to do is to bury the beggar-monk hastily. Later, curious dogs unearth the coffin, and curious people open it, only to discover that there is no body within.

The screen seems to flicker. I know that's impossible. The movie is playing on my computer screen, running off of an old disc. My screen doesn't flicker. It's just too late in the night. My eyes are playing tricks on me.

Three months ago, my aunt died in the aftermath of a stroke. I was told that she was working on the day of the incident. She was found collapsed on the floor shortly after she had made a phone call, and spent the next two weeks or so in a hospital, unconscious, before finally passing away in mid-September. The news hit us all hard. My aunt was 72.

She was gone too soon, but can't the same be said about most people? Or perhaps cliché is the whole point. Seldom are the occasions where death does not come at least somewhat abruptly, somewhat unexpectedly, and in using the phrase, we condition ourselves to a difficult reality.

I've always thought of her as someone who led her life with great energy and direction. These words seem hollow and meaningless as I write them, but they are all I can afford. In her last years, she was committed to social work, and while I was never a part of it, in my mind's eye, I could always see her leading her team with vigour and dedication, doing her best for the elderly in their care. I could still see that stern expression that she wore so often, I could hear her boisterous laugh, these memories without context, soon no longer memories, but ghost-images, purely imagined.

Over the years, I have developed a perhaps obsessive fascination with the film *Center Stage*. The film, directed by Stanley Kwan and starring Maggie Cheung as Ruan Lingyu, perhaps the biggest star of Chinese cinema of her time. Ruan was a silent movie actress who made her name on melodrama films that showcased her expressive acting.

Ruan Lingyu committed suicide at the age of 24. She took an overdose of barbiturates on 8 March 1935. Research cites her deteriorating relationship with her husband as the main factor in her suicide, especially with evidence suggesting that she was physically abused on the night of her death. However, she was also said to have been tormented by the media. The film emphasises this second direction. In fact, her last words in a letter to her husband suggest that she was driven to suicide by gossip.

The film is marked by her death from its first moment, or even before it even begins. Typically, one goes into it knowing full well about Ruan's death, if not of its tragic details. Her death is eschatological, a candle in the dark, a point in the horizon, drawing us into an inevitable destiny. In this sense, every spectatorship experience cannot possess the abruptness or disruptive power of death. Instead, it resembles a prolonging of the wake, a recurring memorial, performed and reperformed, a spectre, or the embers of a fire unable to die.

With my family, I visit the hospital repeatedly over the course of two weeks. As I watch my cousin deal with the impact of my aunt's stroke, I begin to admire his resolve, how he manages to keep it together.

I imagine myself having to take care of the work of death—the nit-ty-gritty details, every phone call, every dollar, every signature—in the event of a loved one's imminent passing, watching as visceral shock transforms into procedures, practices, making some kind of processional sense.

One time, as I tried putting together an essay on the film, I struggled to identify one of the actors. I sought help from different friends, looked up a variety of books, I checked every name in the credits, but came up with nothing. It wasn't surprising. This turbidity, this lack of information, had always characterised my experience of the film.

I first encountered *Center Stage* without having seen any of her films before. Opportunities to see any of these films had always been few and far between. This would be the case for a long time, but eventually, I would come across one or two clips now and then, but there was precious little that I could really count on. All I had was a fragmented picture, or perhaps more accurately, a fragmentary one, something mirrored by Kwan's film. For me, her life took shape from these bits and pieces, and the chasms in between. The gaps, like Sappho's missing words, quickly became a part of my appreciation of her, clarifying absences that gave shape to her unknowability. Yet, in many ways, aren't all encounters delineated by this limit of knowl-edge? Isn't this the condition of every biographical attempt, every friendship, every first date, every last goodbye?

Or perhaps that wasn't my first encounter with the film. The first time I actually remember watching the film, I was engrossed, but as it went on, I started to develop an odd sense of déjà vu. It was only when I reached the final scenes that I realised that I had misremembered. My mind began to fill in the gaps. It wasn't my first encounter, but the point of origin was no longer accessible to me except through imagination.

In one sense, the task of biography is simple narrativisation, both a type of making sense of assorted facts and a process of filling in the gaps. These assemblages sort complex shapes into a thin veneer, something more easily digestible, with more of a semblance of sense. In seeking the memory of something so completely other, we first do violence to the other. We believe in the capacity of the mind to piece together a satisfactory total, imperfect as it is. So perhaps, the only genuine path to biography is one that opens up the possibility of other surfaces, other sheens, one that accepts gaps and errors, the illusion of memory and the impossibility of perfect reproduction.

Shadows.

It is August 2016. The cat is dying. He has been to the clinic multiple times. He has stopped eating for some time, perhaps seeking a particular transformation. We clean him daily. We feed him using a syringe. Nevertheless, his weight has plummeted over the past two months. The vet says that we'll be lucky not to see his condition deteriorate. Realistically, it's only a matter of time. We do our best for him, even if we're not sure if it truly accomplishes anything. Things have become routine, and in their routineness, lose significance. In the process, we learn to let go. At some point, a type of doubling occurs, where he is no longer just our cat but also a dying body.

The questions keep coming. Was it our fault? And if so, what was the point at which it became our fault? Was there a tipping point, a moment? Perhaps it was when we first handed the cat to his adopters. Perhaps it was long before we had even found him out in the streets, perhaps diet, genetics, when we decided to bring him to the vet. Yet, as I continue to turn the thought of it over in my head, I discover that there is no single point of origin, no turn of the screw, no edenic fall, just a complicated, complex weaving of causes leading to one superficial effect.

Soon, he will be just memory. Maybe that process has already begun and it explains the doubling. We must not forget to grieve, for in that moment, the doubling ceases. In mourning, we embrace story, and our friend turns fully into language, into reason, passing into narrative, allowing us to move on.

My sister spent time unearthing photographs that were decades old. My mother too would dig up old pictures. I remember her saying that my aunt used to smile more. Maybe she was happier then. Maybe she was less tired. Or maybe it was just a type of nostalgia.

Things never stop. I went to work as usual. I took the same bus, did the same things, ate the same food. On some days, I went to the hospital after work. On one occasion, my sister came by my office to have lunch. And each time after a hospital visit, the family too would eat together. Meals were comforting. They were opportunities for each of us to show each other that things could be normal again, or simply that there was such a thing as normal after all.

I never looked at a single old photograph, although I kept trying to piece together memories. I didn't trust what I had summoned. The memories were imperfect, or perhaps, too perfect. They were echoes without the illusion of objectivity. Perhaps I preferred it that way.

Zeami, he said, described the art of Nō as the secret of the flower, oblivious to the yellow flame trembling outside the classroom, on the branch, exhausting its poetry, soon negated, nullified, to allow another to speak

anew.

Further outside: well-defined paths, concrete, asphalt, seeming to describe all destinies, and

the tree a deciduous pimple, fractal sideshow, distraction. The eyes on the yellow flame, enable its flickering dance, an unnoticed pinch on the skin of the world casting shadows and creating

time.

The yellow flame knows all deaths are certain, but now, faintly swaying, rich with hesitation, it renders moments with gravity, quivering meaning, sometimes visible, sometimes disappearing, and sometimes gone.

Uncertainty is all.

I have always found it odd that, in English, the film is known as *Center Stage, Actress*, and its Cantonese title of *Yuen Ling-yuk*. At the same time, the film has seen different cuts, and versions with different dubbing. These facts seem to coincide with the fragmentary nature of the film, which cuts back and forth between narrative, interviews, and documentary clips of the production. It is as though there is no best way to begin speaking of her.

This is a form of resistance. The act of recording flattens, conceals, obliterates. The work of editing accomplishes much in making sense and meaning through erasure and transmutation. Reality contorts into a singular text, a sentence. This is the nature of a film, which in itself is a type of writing. Should the film adopt a dramatic narrative as its approach, it will fail. Instead, it needs to resist the lure of convention, of sense. To capture the complexities of Ruan's life, it needs to defy the nature of its tools and find performance.

It continues to play. The scene moves on without me. Arguably the most famous one of the film, it restages a scene from *New Women* (1934), one of her last movies. Set in what appears to be a hospital ward, Ruan—as played by Maggie Cheung—appears to be in poor health. As it develops, we find that Ruan is merely playing a character on-set. Here, the film concentrates on the body of the performer. The repeated use of close-ups brings it into frame. Ruan/Cheung's face often becomes the sole focus of the shots. The sharp contrast of the performer's face and the plainness of the costume and set design intensifies the focus on the body. The lighting too seems to place her in the spotlight. Whimpers and gasps, all stressing the proximity to the performer's body. In more dramatic exchanges, the way in which her voice falters in desperation, the sound of her struggling to breathe, and the uncontrolled—perhaps uncontrollable—sobbing once again betray the body, insisting on its presence beyond the mere act of signification.

Then, the camera pulls back. Stanley Kwan's voice is heard, and the image of the director appears on-screen. He refers to the actors by name. This move reveals the film as a constructed thing, a filmic text. Cheung's immediate performance, recorded, absorbed into an edited film, is gone. The actor's body has vanished. There is nothing left but a flat signifier.

This is why the film has to seek performance, to become a stable text in search of an unstable moment. It is less about the comprehensive recovery of facts—the objective, the stable, the body—than it is about transition from material complexity to shallow signifier— the transient, the performance, the unutterable. *Ruan Lingyu* is not an attempt to accurately portray the life of the actress as much as it is a staging of its inevitable failure to do so. Inevitable, for what sort of biopic would do her life justice? How could a film possibly explain a subject so intricate and vast? Take, for example, the motivation behind her suicide. In the film, she is driven to her death by gossip rags and the paparazzi, whereas contemporary opinion emphasises her deteriorating relationship with her husband and the possibility of domestic violence. Yet, who is to say that either had more sway than the other?

In the final scenes, Ruan is seen penning her suicide note, a detail which has been brought into question over the years. Regardless of its accuracy, the scene depicts her warning that words—gossip—can be frightful. I used to think that it was a facile form of moralising, but now it becomes clear to me that it is a part of the greater thesis of the film, a statement that we can never access the internal complexities of her life, of anyone's life, of anything in particular. Its own acts of remembrance—and ours—are limited by the inaccessibility of the past. Things have already happened, their substance decayed. No, the film's focus on hearsay and scandal is a quite deliberate means of scaffolding its larger theme of representation and the recuperation of truth. What are gossip and rumour, after all, but attempts at turning painfully incomplete flashes of truth into coherent stories? The processes and intent may be different, but they resemble the film's efforts insofar as they struggle to put together the story of Ruan Lingyu, struggling to cohere.

This is our disease. We cannot resist the narrativisation of reality. We cannot resist the lure of signs and stories. Language seduces, and through language, material reality loses its abundant presence, solidifying into sentences, sense.

On the Thursday after the news first hit, I took out a book of poetry by José Ángel Valente, translated by Thomas Christensen[1]. Expecting the worst, I sought comfort in words. I imagined drama in the first lines: "I must die. And yet, nothing/dies, because nothing/has enough faith to be able to die." I imagined resilience, defiance, fortitude.

There is a sense of purpose in these words. "I must die", they say. I must, as though that is the purpose of living. This isn't a new argument—we have always known to seek a good death—but the energy of these words propels the poem towards this confrontation.

This would be the poem that I would count on for the following days, going over it again and again, meditating upon its meanings, its possibilities, drawing it into encounters with different moments, a constant recontextualisation. Perhaps appropriately, for the second part of the poem is: "The day does not die/it passes;/nor a rose,/it fades;/the sun sets,/it does not die." These lines describe a circularity to nature, and to my mind, they are charged with emotion. Is it celebration or discontentment?

Human life has the form of a sentence or story, beginning, middle and end. However, only in juxtaposing the circular against the linear, only in seeking performance in the vast repetition of life does meaning truly take shape. So, finally: "Only I, who have touched/the sun, the rose, the day,/and have thought,/I can die."

Sometime in 2017, I went to catch a restored version of *Love and Duty*, starring Ruan Lingyu, with a colleague. The screening was held in the auditorium of a local museum during a weekend. I went in uncertain of what to expect. I think I was nervous. Another one of the gaps was about to be filled, and it would distort whatever picture of her I had imagined.

Each time her face flashed across the screen, it was shining, this luminous ghost, a perfect sign, a total representation yet limited in dimensions. Isn't it strange how a film survives after the fact? Its basis is acting, the immediate and visceral, and yet every film exists in the afterlife of the performance, recorded, edited, reproduced, a body becoming text. Yet it is the visceral—the body, the senses, the grain of the voice—that we seek. This incongruity lies at the heart of *Center Stage*. The central drama of the film is Maggie Cheung's struggle to produce an authentic performance that matches the reality of life, and by extension, the documenter's inability to produce a stable truth. Cheung is drawn into the performance, forcefully swept into the life of another, the absence of the other, and as such the separation between performance and fact dissolves. All bodies transform into signs, all lives into stories, but between film and gossip, Ruan dies and lives on, incandescent, insubstantial, inscrutable.

One day it finally happened. She had led a good life, but it still felt cruel. I can't remember if it was raining. Perhaps it was. Yes, it was, and the rain fell without a sound, without colour or

    texture

        without purpose

    sodden void, drowned ending

    nothing possible

    no transformations.

Each of them walked through the doors as though they had rehearsed. They came in, signed in the book, saw the body, gave their condolences, and sat at the tables.

A colleague of mine, the same one that had watched the movie, came with his partner to the wake as a gesture of solidarity. I sat with them through the proceedings. We were mostly quiet, though, to be fair, what could they possibly have said? We sat among the stories, observing. I wanted to tell them stories of my own, but I couldn't find the words. I suppose that I felt that I couldn't tell them anything they hadn't already figured out.

They left before too long, but I remained among the voices. One of my younger cousins, who worked with her in social work, delivered a eulogy. His words were heartfelt, and they sketched my aunt in detail. I realised then that these words helped to draw things to a close. Like every other story about my aunt told within the hall, they contained no communicative value intrinsically. They did not tell us anything we didn't already know or expect. There was nothing to be learned. Yet, the words themselves were a dedication, a way of saying, I remember you so.

The stories are merely tools, incantations, repetitions against senselessness, even if they are unfair representations, lacking in detail, exactness. The simple action of repeating these stories is comforting. Certainly, they gloss over things unfairly, but they are our only recourse, as we seek not so much the other, but a chance to perform ourselves, to remember the ineffable moment of encounter and the lasting truths outside of words. What we seek is not accuracy or truth value, but something beyond language, and perhaps beyond simple representation.

There they spent their entire evening, constantly battering themselves against the glass and impotent fire, incessantly, futilely, charging towards the electric light, coming from which there could be nothing. Perhaps they sought to discover their solitude or that moment when they first discovered humans. Or perhaps they sought death in the affirmation of fire. Wasn't it a beggar-monk who in that old story disembowels himself?

At the end of the film, Ruan Lingyu's body lies motionless. It is a scene at the wake. But it is a false body—images, data. The director shouts cut. Maggie Cheung opens her eyes, and takes a breath.

I walk along in a line, shuffling along with the other members of my family. As though intruding on a photograph, I place a flower in near her left wrist. The death of a person begins from the moment we meet them, and it is completed when we grieve. A ghost is nothing more than a story, but it may be all we can muster. We must mourn, but we must also not forget that there was once a body, there was blood, breathing.

Still, the screen seems to flicker. The film has ended. Ruan has transformed, her body no longer remains. Only its image remains, impervious to our voyeuristic gazes. All that remains are stories. Is this why the theme song of the film—its title literally meaning a burial of the heart—states that when the swallows of spring return, the body can no longer be found?

Time and again, I watch the film. I am seeking my own moments. We narrate our stories to preserve our memories, but we must become aware of the divide between word and moment, between object and subject, between sign and event. We must actively pursue encounter and reencounter, time and again, to defy narrativisation and language.

Every text is a postscript, always already written, a ghost of the performance, or perhaps a scar, a corpse. Every photograph is an extrusion of a moment, a pure echo of the sensory surface through which we experience the world. Every film. Every sight. Each sound. Our scars are the memories that we carry, continue to carry, narratives that signify across time, impervious, untouched. Yet, they are robbed of their substance, removed from the wound, impressions without bodies.

How should we exist between the stability of narrativisation and the need for mourning? In this constant negotiation between substance and surface, perhaps through our stories—impossible as it may be—we seek small moments, miniscule spaces where there can be the possibility of renewal. Language itself is unstable, prone to splits, doublings, voids and vacancies. Through writing, image, logic, picture, sound, we speak anew, attendant to the gaps, the ambiguities, telling the same old stories, but seeking new possibilities, thought without discourse, goodbyes without words, language without language.

It was morning. Perhaps it was morning. Perhaps I sat at my front door. Perhaps it rained. Yes, let's say that it rained. The rain was heavy yesterday when I sat in front of my door. Gradually, it began to diminish, although I only realised when it had stopped, perhaps insensitive, perhaps in sync. Something flickered, something stirred. In the distance, a cat walked across the street. A seed sprouts unseen. Quiet, stillness. Sun.

Were you there? Yes, either real or imagined, both real and imagined. And we sat, holding hands, unknown and unknowable to each other, thinking of the passing days, of every friend and story, both the living and the dead, and too aware of the secret of the flower, transient, infinitesimal, total, conscious of each moment, or perhaps conscious of the cascade of moments, each instant split into further instants, and in this microcosm, we perceive, just barely, the infinite sense of time, our infinite performance, rendered invisibly, framed by death, departures,

not a cinder not a sound

CINDERS
2017, 2018, 2020, 2022

)

Tomorrow I will write you again, in our
foreign language. I won't remember a word
of it and in September, without my having
even seen it again, you will burn,

you will burn it,
it has to be you.

Derrida

ONE ■ The Failure Artist

> 7 April 2020. On the first day, there is an almost biblical
> rain that seems to reset the world. For the next eight
> weeks, I barely step out of the house. Trapped at home, I
> begin to review my back pages.

In *The Universal Translation Machine*, a comically stereotypical mad scientist creates a device capable, of course, of translating any language into another. Like some aberrant retelling of Babel, this absurd technology drives civilisation to great new heights of community and cooperation, while also resulting in great reckonings. This fable ends with a group of individuals who, having finally found the means to engage with dialogue with their consciences, now sit forever in silence.

In *Invisibility*, an unnamed man is on-board a train crossing a channel when he finds himself gradually vanishing. There is a suggestion that he has sacrificed much to get here, that this ticket to a new life has come at a great cost. At first, he panics as he watches the invisibility travel slowly across his body, but, as though overtaken by resignation or apathy, soon calms down. The man begins to realise that he will never see his own face again, that he will forget the limits of his own body. His family too will soon forget his existence. He wonders if his ability to speak to—and speak of—the visible world will soon be compromised. As he takes on his new job, he will gradually grow accustomed to being unseen and unheard. The entire episode is resolved in acceptance as he embraces his invisibility. As the train rumbles on, he wonders how many more of such individuals have crossed the channel and become invisible too.

Genericity of Rejections mimics a series of text messages between two people in the aftermath of a failed romantic confession. The exchange becomes increasingly absurd, with one party playing like a Shakespearean fool. Cynical and slightly mean-spirited, it picks at the notion that all rejections are mundane and cannot possibly mean anything.

There are a lot of these false starts—and even non-starts. One time some years ago, insistent on a type of ironic, cannibalising art, this became the basis of a cynically acidic take on creative failure. I wrote *Digression*, a novella about a young writer who one day receives a returned manuscript for a novel that he is supposed to have written. He reads the manuscript and it strikes him as something he would have written when he was much younger, except that he has no memory of ever doing so. One thing leading to another, the paranoid protagonist starts to believe that someone has appropriated his identity for nefarious reasons and becomes obsessed about tracking down this criminal, only to one day encounter a person with his voice, with his face.

The narrative takes place post facto, and the titular digression refers chiefly to the protagonist's refusal to confront the memory of the encounter. Trying to fend it off, he is inevitably led back to it, merely taking the long way round in his musings about the archetype of the double in art and media, from José Saramago to Lord Byron, from *The Double Life of Veronique* to *Kagemusha*. This would eventually become the short story *Dark Matter*, a much more to-the-point and marginally more effective stab at the same premise.

When the pandemic begins, I start to have uncharacteristically vivid dreams. One night, I dream of dancers in some quiet, immovable darkness, illuminated by embers, twirling and pirouetting, with perfect control of their bodies, spinning, muscular machinery, twirling, the motion of the universe.

For a time, I became obsessed with writing about what I can only describe as idiosyncratic disease. These fictional diseases were sometimes physical, sometimes phenomenological, but a consistent feature was how these characters were alone in their suffering. In retrospect, I was probably at the age where I was interested in feelings of alienation, and such diseases felt like a way of bringing out the isolation and sense of alienation that characterised modern life.

There was one titled *Nausea*, in which the protagonist suffers from an intense and inexplicable nausea on his way to the airport, an extreme depiction of an existentially terrifying anonymity that would sometimes grip me during travel. On the other hand, there was one—*Bloom*—in which a father grows a third eye, causing him incredible consternation for an entire morning, before realising that an even greater transformation has been taking place before his very eyes, as his infant child begins taking her first steps.

Cognition's discomfort was subtler and certainly much more challenging to write about effectively. It concentrated on a man for whom the very definitions of left and right, up and down have been swapped, resulting in an unnerving and unnameable existential malady.

The Tain was about a child who grew up with no reflection.

The longest of these pieces was *Minor Illusions*, a story about a man who starts losing the ability to perceive faces, a strange illness which I initially named Metzger's Disease and then later Mizumura Syndrome because I had a copy of a book by the writer Minae Mizumura at my desk. The character was transparently called Darryl.

One time, so invested in this narrative of failure, I wrote a proposal for an exhibition called *Seven Failures by Peter Lai*, centred around the work of a fictional writer and artist, the titular Peter Lai. The proposal was fuelled by my obsession with the work of Roberto Bolaño at the time, and I was keen most of all to make a dramatic character whose failures made for the best literature.

I wake up and find a key in my mouth. I have never seen it before. At first, I am startled, but this feeling dissipates, leaving only a desperate urgency to unravel its mystery. To no avail, I check every lock in the house. And so, I venture into the city. It's night. The breeze is unnatural, and the stars are brighter than they should be. I try every lock I find along the street, and then the next one, and the next, the next. My footsteps grow hurried, my breathing erratic. Before long, I remember everything about the key: its shape, its size, its metallic sheen, its temperature. The completeness of these details frightens me. And as I move from one failed attempt to the next, the key becomes the only thing that my mind can contain. I see a woman down the street. I approach and try to ask for help, but I fail to speak. There are no words left. Out of compassion or sympathy, she nods and walks away. In despair, without language, I return the key to my mouth.

I wake in a sweat. It is only another dream. Alarmingly, I find the same key in my mouth. It feels familiar in my hand. The panic subsides. I realise that it is merely the key to this place in which I have always been locked.

The Inventors was a novel about a few fictional writers in Singapore, all larger than life, all romantic and idealised, as well as the ordinary lives around them. In retrospect, I must have felt constrained by my limited talent and in my frustration, created a wild fictional space that spoke to an aspirational literature. It was a youthful endeavour.

I borrowed many of the characters from earlier projects. In a sense, I danced around with the same characters for years, continuing to revisit them time and again. They were indulgent characters, and over time I came to realise they often drew directly from my internal voice. You should never put too much of yourself into your work. Many times, they satisfied only an internal logic, like an inside joke or an insipid secret, unable to communicate, unable to cohere.

The novel did not survive. Vaguely, I had an impression even as I was writing that it would go nowhere. It was not the first time. I repeated this cycle several times over the years, producing meaningless work that would satisfy no one, not even myself. I don't know why I persisted. Since childhood I had been designated the writer among classmates and family members, and I toiled endlessly to live up to it, foolishly undertaking project after project, hoping that something would bear fruit. I must have written close to a million words. A specialist in failure.

I first encountered Neil Gaiman's *The Sandman* at a young age. Inspired by its gripping plot and use of mythology, I spent several years foolishly trying to reproduce a similar effect in my writing. I often cribbed directly from things I loved at that age, but it always led to disaster as I blindly attempted to imitate the methods without any understanding of the craftsmanship that underpinned the creation of these works. I believed myself perfectly equipped to tackle mythopoeia in my writing. I was also 15 and lacked both craft and craftiness.

I wrote a short novel called *The River*. An absurd gangland drama with a cockamamie plot set in Singapore, it featured star-crossed lovers who naïvely compared their plight to myth and fable. It was an immature creation, but I sometimes look back at it and think that I've yet to move on from the same thematic obsessions to this day, that even then I already had some inkling of the human addiction to mythmaking and storytelling.

> 2 May 2020. I write furiously. It comes as a response
> to everything that is happening around me. An urge to
> vent, a release valve. Yet the more that I write, the more

it becomes clear that there is very little that I am saying. My writing deteriorates. There were those that I hoped to amplify, but the voice flattens out into empty noise. I'm projecting, I'm misreading, I'm exploiting, I'm irresponsibly vocalising. I try to find silence. I write myself into wordlessness.

TWO ■ Float

A memory: How are you? she asked. Not good, I said. A look of surprise. I supposed that the answer was not what she had expected. But I didn't know what else I was supposed to say.

Trapped in a wordless limbo, I retreated into the smaller work of how-are-you. I reached out to friends actively, seeking connections with people near and far, trying to engage with people I was close to or had drifted far from. At the time, I had yet to understand this work often consisted of hollow gestures. Perhaps I sought comfort, some sort of consolation. I didn't realise how little I could do, and didn't anticipate how, no matter how well-meaning I was, it could all feel as though I was expressing empathy to make myself feel better. And yet, it seemed like all I could muster.

After flailing about for a while doing this work, my words felt dilute. I understood that sometimes our narratives fail us, and that how-are-you's are the stories that we tell ourselves.

Every so often I would step away from it all, from work, from writing, from social connections. It helped me to focus on the small things, the immediate things, the people and spaces around me.

I became concerned about my mother. There was nothing outwardly worrying, but it was clear to me that living in the same house had become taxing now that she had to suddenly include my father and I round the clock in her daily life. Her space had certainly contracted. Time too must have taken on a different structure. I wondered if she was tired, if she needed more from us, if the lockdown had caused disappointments and interruptions in her life that she had to untangle.

It ought to have been the simplest of questions, but as though unwilling to shatter an illusion or unmask some precious secret, I struggled. In fact, I never did ask. I came to realise that between Mother's life and mine was a vast chasm. That is, I would have to understand so much of her I did not know before, her hopes and aspirations, her stories and histories, her joys and miseries—and not just superficially either. These things seemed to me towering in their impossibility. There is only so much we can communicate and so much we can understand. It alarmed me how a mother and child—the closest of all relationships—could see the years come between them. I fell into despair.

We ask the question so carelessly, but true how-are-you's are a confrontation with the absoluteness of otherness.

Outside, the world churns. News of so much suffering.

Reverberations from distant places. It churns even when it's quiet.

During my university years, I became enamoured with theatre and performance, to the point where I daydreamed about developing productions of my own. Despite having no training at all, I developed a yearning to create a play.

The play of my dreams was going to be titled《你還好嗎？》—How are you? How have you been?—a simple tale of two former university classmates bumping into each other several years later at a park bench. It would feature essentially these two characters, with each played by three actors. The two characters would trade stories about themselves since they last met, with the other actors re-enacting the stories that were being told behind the bench. The actors would rotate, taking turns to become narrator and reenactors, both stories and storytellers. Unfolding as a series of tall tales and unexpected truths, it would be a play about the human tendency to exaggerate, to boast, to fabricate, to reassure, and to evade. I didn't know it then, but it was about how difficult it was to answer the question of how are you.

I wanted it to end the way it started, with nothing but a bench and a tree, because for a time I was obsessed with the idea that performance was capable of a type of perfect art—one that left no traces. I never acted on my fascination with drama because the barrier of entry always seemed much too high.

Our cat begins waking people up at 6.30am every

morning, then 7am.

My office hours shift, starting later, ending earlier, until we must all telecommute.

It becomes impossible to promise anything, to plan anything.

Father becomes increasingly confused by everyday realities, as though slowly succumbing to some chaotic daze in his mind.

Overseas trips are cancelled, no further ones imaginable.

I wonder sometimes how the elderly look at this dwindling year. I wonder what my parents are about each passing day.

As the pandemic develops across the globe, I tell myself ghost stories.

When my grandmother died in 2019, the ordeal left so little within me, and I carried an emptiness within for several months. I felt as though I had kept putting off the work of acceptance and letting go, and this continued after her death. I kept myself busy with writing, with social engagements, with life, everything but the work of mourning.

As panic sweeps across the globe, I find myself thinking of her. Sometimes I wonder about what she would think had she returned just briefly after her departure, to a world so vastly different from the one she had left behind, characterised by sudden disruptions and long-overdue awakenings. Sometimes I would dream of her confusion as she stood along the empty rain-slicked streets.

For her, it's like the story never ended. The last thing she remembers is the face of the helper who was her primary caregiver in the last days of her life. And now, there are only lonely streets and deserted stores, masks on faces and coloured tape on seats. Now, there is only dreadful quiet or billowing unrest, a world she doesn't understand—as though she's missed a chapter.

Like with the spectre that returns to Hamlet, we know that all ghosts are stories and all stories are glitches in time.

> 21 April 2020. Some days, I look out the window and it is striking to me how it all looks like a scene from a film. Gripped by silence, the world seems to have turned a page. An eschatological vision, like the aftermath of some great flood, some apocalypse, some premature denouement.

Like that scene at the end of *The Beyond*.

Zombie films—and horror films in general—thrive on genre expectations, but I remember my first encounter with Lucio Fulci's *The Beyond* taking me by surprise. It exceeded the conventions of its genre, deploying familiar tropes and archetypes, yet flirting with greater aesthetic and narrative ambitions. To me, the final scene of the film has always epitomised this in how it stretches the limits of expression of the genre. The scene has two characters emerging from the zombie-infested corridors of a hospital and walking into a thick fog that has blanketed the city. Few are the zombie movies that reach beyond the realm of the grotesque and venture into the metaphysical in such audacious fashion. In effect, *The Beyond* travels from bodily violence to a purgatory devoid of society—itself a system of manmade meaning—becoming timeless, mythological.

Every rendition of purgatory is a portrayal of a reality without time. Time sheds its common meaning in the event of catastrophe, but this catastrophe dissolves into perpetuity and deathlessness, the utter failure of time. The zombie itself is a representation of such perpetuity, a bodily eternity without any concept of death, a past that persists without a future.

The Beyond traces the decline of civilisation in the event of a disaster into a fog where all meaning is lost because the vanished time makes nothing possible. Language is frozen, unable to adequately describe the immensity of eternity or the incalculable scale of the disaster, but also faced with the prospect of eventually running itself out. Without change or event, there is only space for one lasting narrative. Much in the same way, even the gruesome violence so crucially a part of the film's aesthetic loses its import in the endgame of *The Beyond*. In the immensity of the fog, each act becomes stifled, snuffed out, silenced within an oppressive grey. There remains nothing but a paralysis of meaning.

Ours is a universe of change, but it is not hard to imagine such change burning out in the cosmic scale of things, leading to a moment, the last moment, that which forever endures, where the underlying indifference of reality becomes undeniable, and our words and actions can no longer inhabit expression.

The true nature of catastrophe is the destruction of meaning, and so we turn to narrative, stories big and small, our desperate attempts to restore some semblance of order, careless, reckless. We check in with others to ground ourselves. But time fails, language

falters.

THREE ■ Void

The pandemic exposes the most vulnerable segments of society, but there is something particularly vicious about this outbreak with its unique combination of rapidity, invisibility, and isolation. At the same time, the virus is, contradictorily, supervisible. Every headline, every social media post. For a time, all faces are undeniably masks, all coughs and sniffles some grim harbinger. As it develops, the pandemic also drags entrenched issues of inequality, violence, exploitation and prejudice into reckoning.

On my part, I feel urgently that I had to do something, and yet, it also feels as though I am not in a position to write about so much of what is unfolding—I lack knowledge, I lack skill, I am an outsider to so much of what is going on. The failure of the artist as middleman, perpetually an outsider, neither interpreter nor intermediary, neither vessel nor voice.

20 May 2020. These days it alternates between scorching
weather and relentless rain. I wake to overcast skies. At
lunchtime, the sun casts its glare on everything outside
the window. Then, by the late afternoon, torrents.

Once, some years ago, no longer content with the mediocre fictions I
had been fashioning and developing over the course of many years, I
decided to wipe the slate clean and start over from nothing. I did not,
however, let go of my love of the mythopoeic. Foolishly believing that
I had enough experience in my writing practice by this time, I sought
to turn perhaps the most well-known Singaporean fable, the tale of
Bukit Merah, into an epic fantasy novel.

In brief, it tells of an island in a season of terror, as hordes of
garfish attack the fishermen and villagers relentlessly. Racking his
brains to little avail, the sultan summons all his military might to fend
off the fish, but this too does not succeed. One day, a young boy from
the village seeks an audience with the sultan. The boy suggests using
banana tree trunks to create a barricade lining the coast. The sultan
agrees to this plan. With the barricade in place, the attacking garfish
find their bills piercing only plant matter. Worse, they are caught
in the barricade with no recourse. The sultan orders his soldiers to
slaughter the fish, thus putting an end to the crisis. The villagers
celebrate the young boy as a hero. Afraid that his throne is under
threat, the sultan hatches a frightening plan to deal with the child. In
the dead of night, the boy is captured by soldiers and murdered atop
a hill. His blood stains the hill red, hence giving Bukit Merah ("red

hill") its name.

My first attempt was a meandering and childish attempt at incorporating fantasy into fable. Thereafter, stumbling through re-write after rewrite and confronted with my inability to tell this tale, I abandoned the manuscripts completely and started from scratch. By that time, I had developed a fascination with the idea that stories existed outside of time, that as soon as they had passed into myth, they would persist. I realised then that I wanted to explore the trans-formation of real people and real things—real violence—into symbol and signification, the flattening of reality into the stories that we tell ourselves. Failing to tell the tale, I decided to emphasise the untellable nature of the tale. I turned to a literature of failure. In the new short story, I interrogated the archetypes of heroism and tragedy, convinced that invited great violence into reality by turning things into narrative vehicles. Further, as it had been told to me, it almost seemed to gloss over the violence embedded in our difficult relationship with nature.

Stories can sometimes be the ultimate violence.

I first came across this line in a *New Yorker* article by Alastair Reid:
"Borges used to say that when writers die they become books—a quite satisfactory incarnation in his view."[1]
but the truth is, all of us become stories eventually. Our realness is fleeting.

When the crisis explodes and severe measures are taken to control the spread of the disease, boredom becomes a sudden and not-unimportant problem. Video games seem uniquely suited to fill this void. Many turn to the comforting virtual world of *Animal Crossing*, where they move to an island with a few other inhabitants and live out daily life in what is essentially a rural village. On its twin engines of charm and customisation, it offers an incredibly potent mix of comfort and control, which are hard to come by in such difficult days. My sister buys me a copy of the game, and encouraged by the game's popular reception, I too dive into its colourful and pleasant world.

In a daily ritual lasting up to exactly a year, I check into my island and undertake the gamut of chores, making sure that I missed no major events or items. Having no facility for great creativity with landscaping or interior design, my island proves to always be a bit of a mess, filled with more visual puns and unfunny jokes for visitors to discover than any intentional design. I spend most of my time futilely tidying up the space, picking fruit and plucking weeds diligently, doing the occasional bit of fishing, and updating the décor from time to time. The drudgery is intoxicating.

As the days go by, I begin to feel the tedium of routine and the tepid envy of seeing much more well-furnished and well-designed islands. *Animal Crossing* is work hidden underneath a veneer of play. Each check-in is a crossed-off number on the calendar. Each new furnishing or design or garden plot represents time and energy spent in this virtual world. As such, it is also a measure of time, anchoring us in an age where time is out of joint.

Seeking a more visceral, a more story driven experience, I turn to the 2019 remake of classic zombie video game *Resident Evil 2*, in which players primarily play as Leon Kennedy and Claire Redfield as they make their way through Raccoon City as it is being overrun by both zombies and an assortment of other frightening creatures. The irony of playing a game about an outbreak during an outbreak is unintentional, but perhaps subconsciously I sought something cathartic.

Resident Evil 2 keeps the player on their toes using a combination of resource scarcity, relentless enemies, and unsettling atmosphere. These are common pillars of survival horror games, and the franchise has also not shied away from other popular narrative clichés. For instance, the basis of *Resident Evil*'s zombie crises is the spread of a virus manufactured by an irresponsible corporation, unfortunately mirroring real-life conspiracy theories that surface as the pandemic blooms. Indeed, the distrust of organisations, acts of espionage, and seeming powerlessness of most individuals mirrors much that is unfolding in real life. Our stories are derived from reality, but they in turn inform reality, a constant cycle of listening and telling, an economy that feeds itself, like some vision of ouroboros, some perpetual motion machine.

As he sits in the classroom confronted by a horrifying educational video,

> in the aftermath of a near fatal traffic accident,
>> upon hearing of a ghastly atrocity,
> he tries to speak.

The boy quickly learns that the voice is the biological response to that which horrifies us. But sometimes there are no words. Sometimes, just silence. Sometimes guttural noises. Sometimes frightened laughter.

> Every now and then, there is such anger that I write furiously, in loud keyboard strokes or uncontrolled scrawls, writing that feels like fire, but also, like fire, burns out quickly, into ash, into nothingness.

Resident Evil's indulgent fiction provides something of an antidote. Heroic narratives such as this appeal to us perhaps because they have the allure of agency or idealisation. They give us the sense that someone can simply come along and turn things around, releasing us from our culpability in the expansive crises of our time. But heroes of this sort aren't real. They are an irresponsible fantasy. They often celebrate the best among us, give us reason to hope, but they also have the potential to absolve, obscure, and erase.

Chinese singer Hua Chenyu's 《鬥牛》—"Bullfighting"— begins with the dramatisation of bullfighting before pivoting into an environmental thesis. The performance of the song blends soaring vocals, furious rap, gnarled growls, and pained cries. In the video— directed by Mitsunori Yokobori, with visual effects by Yuhei Kanbe of Perimetron— Hua strikes several poses that evoke the bullfighting context symbolically. (In fact, the cape movement of the Veronica is repeatedly referenced in the lyrics.) Through a combination of CGI, illustration, and filmed segments, the video paints the cruelty of this human romanticisation in evocative tones of black, red, and white. There are visions of robotic bullfights, shrouded figures with the ghastly painted smiles participating in the violence, soulless cities, bodies drifting towards the sky, and then burning forests, melting ice.

The awfulness of bullfighting encapsulates a central problem in our relationship with the environment. We are conditioned to anthropocentric modes of storytelling, where there are values such as heroism, courage, valour, and virtue, values that do not apply to the world around us. Juxtaposing the romanticised appeal of a blood sport against our worsening environmental situation, the song and its video suggest that our tendencies towards anthropocentrism has a detrimental effect on ourselves. As an abstract, computer-generated bull corpse transforms into an abstract, computer-generated human body, it becomes clear that our stories inform the world at large, and thus can constitute a violence that we render unto the other, our reality, and ultimately ourselves.

Perhaps this reading is too simplistic. Humans have a tremendous capacity for blindness, for forgetting. It is the self-centredness at the heart of it all—as a species, as a community, as individuals—that allows us to speak irresponsibly. We like to tell stories about the big things, about our rapidly deteriorating environment, about lofty ideals of altruism and chivalry, about success or achievement or genius, because these stories also allow us false assurances, also enable us to reinforce divisions, also empower our collective inaction. Writing, storytelling, invention can be dangerous without the direction, structure, and imperative of moral responsibility.

He doesn't have the words. He sees the news, the labels, the divisions, the unbuilt bridges, but cannot find a way to speak. Hollow. All hollow. Upon this realisation, the world contracts suddenly and violently for him. In a fit, he writes, crudely constructing pieces without purpose or end, like howling at the storm.

As the pandemic settles into our lives, I begin to develop a terrible fear. What sort of world are we going to inhabit when the dust settles? Will time revert to its former shape? Will we find isolation or solidarity in the aftermath? What will happen to our values? To our systems of governance? It isn't the uncertainty that frightens me. It is a fear of amnesia, that collectively, we will forget the lessons that this crisis has taught us, lessons about the way we treat one another, about inequality, about excess, swiftly and wilfully returning to lives of cruelty and destruction. I worry that it will all fade away, burn out after this awful firestorm. I don't fear disruption, downturn, or grief as much as I fear amnesia.

> 4 June 2020. For the first time in nearly three months, I
> feel the rain on my skin again.

But we do forget. Things rapidly overtake our efforts to remember. We celebrate the return of the Olympics, lament inflationary prices, watch as powerful factions march into war or continue to wage it. And with enough time, these things will be forgotten too. Our capacity to forget is critical to our penchant for both cruelty and self-destruction.

The panic of two years ago seems so distant now. We forget how the world had changed. (Has it really?) We forget the anger of days past. (Anger never lasts.) We forget the people we left behind. (We just continue to leave them behind.)

All that is left are these words, these scars.

FOUR ■ Hollows

But cinders can also be resilient.

Sometimes I still believe in a perfect art, one that erases all trace of itself. I am no longer convinced, however, that it is purely an aesthetic exercise.

> 25 June 2020. I keep struggling to write about the pandemic. I keep failing. My back pages are a patchwork of failures that enables this work.

We can write to illuminate,

to allow others the light in which to lead us into their worlds.
We can write to find the courage to ask, to find

the invitation of how are you.

We can tell tales carefully, manufacture fictions that strive to enable the vulnerable.

We can fail to tell tales, to try again and again, retellings in a sea of retellings, definitions and redefinitions.

And even if we don't succeed, even if we fail to properly ask how are you, even if there are no words left, it is essential that we keep trying.

We can write to erase ourselves. It is okay to burn up in the service of others.

The emptiness is a space
in which silenced voices may settle
and grow.

FIVE ■ Envois

Woman, will you hear the story of my dreams?

Oh shut up.

It's important.

You never have anything important to say.

There is truth in these dreams.

So you've said.

Is it because you doubt me? Do you doubt what I've seen? But I dream again and again, and as you know, repetition is the basis of all reality. There is substance to these visions, truth in my slumber, percolating into some form of future. Perhaps it is already written. Perhaps our paths are set. Premonitions must draw their shape from some type of memory, all information must have a source, the future must already have happened.

Of course I have my doubts. It is a woman's nature to doubt and a man's to regret.

Wasn't it Shakespeare who wrote that our doubts are traitors and make us lose the good we oft might win?

I believe so, but he hasn't been born yet, so perhaps it isn't true yet. It wouldn't make sense for something that has yet to happen to prove to be true. Things take time. Or perhaps it would only make sense to someone outside of time, a god, a fundamental force, or an angel of history. An outsider.

You know that I have an irrational fear of eavesdroppers.

Surely someone somewhere must be listening, undetected, undisturbed.

Why doesn't this certainty absolve us of the fear? Woman, I prefer to deal with things I can see, touch, and remember. I can trust them.

Stop being so simple. We've been here before. I can't help but feel we've been here before. All right then, I'll indulge you, only because I always do. So tell me, then. Tell me again of your dreams.

Thank you, but now I'm scared of doing so. I'm afraid I'll speak it into existence.

Make up your mind.

I'm just scared. Can't you understand?

You're always scared, but you seem so convinced of their truth, and if you're this sure about anything, then hasn't it already happened? Aren't all visions of the future written in the past?

True. I suppose there is nothing I can do to change things.

Then, speak. Take that load off your mind.

It's dark.

It is.

It starts in the twilight, along the tranquil shore, within the gentle sea. Then an ill wind arises, the waters stir, unnatural and swift, the fishing-people are killed in a senseless violence, silver creatures rising from the water, larger than men, their bills piercing hearts and lungs, a sea of swords and then a sea of brackish blood. And I saw in the continued massacre of the people their tormented faces, fists still clenched, eyes bloodshot, faces pale, souls lost, severed from their remaining days. Then, portraits of grieving families, pictures, sketches, lines, anguished like scribbles, senseless lines unable to return to their original shapes.

Twelve days of bloodshed.

Amid this anguish, a boy seeks an audience with the frightened king.

Our son. Just tell it straight. It's our son.

Unable to stomach further deaths, the boy intends to put forth a plan, and the desperate ruler cannot turn away even a sliver of hope. The child and the king exchange words in the sullen morning. Outside, one faintly hears the distant sounds of crows descending and picking at the carcasses. The boy's plan is audacious, but with despair exceeding caution, the king agrees to it. He orders troops to gather banana tree trunks, from which they create a barricade. They work through the night and prop up the barricade along the shore. Then they wait for daybreak.

When the morning comes, a few men wade into the waters as

bait. The fish emerge from the waves, and strike at the barricade mindlessly. The trap is sprung. Their bills pierce through the plant matter with little trouble, but they fail to wrest themselves free thereafter. A tide of men charge towards the fish, desperate to avenge their kin. One massacre transforms into another, murder across the cape of stakes, men with swords and smiles gleaming, striking with sickening glee, addicted to the dark taste of revenge. As the clang of metal dies down and the waters settle... Crowds, then voices, then cheering, figures wild with joy, feet steeped in the blood of their enemies.

Across the island, there are days of festivities, nights singing and drinking, a people drunk on their undeserved happiness. But the king abstains, finding himself disturbed by the increasing celebrity of the child. One day, in the heat of the afternoon, the king is jolted awake by his fears. Certain that the boy will soon be a threat to his throne, he orders an assassination.

I know the rest.

I must go on.

Don't.

The soldiers are faceless, shadows that march through the thickening night. They surround the village, then, an attempt at escape, fleet footsteps, the shapes dissolve, leaving nothing but an amorphous, ominous shadow. Desperate breathing, nervous footsteps, howling wind, silhouettes marching up the slope of the hill. The moment approaches, a frightened face, a blade and a flash in the dead of night, the gush of blood, a staunched scream, a dull thud, and then the hill, and then red.

Look how you cower, look how you quiver and shake at the thought of some inevitable destiny, your face shrivelled, your voice flagging, your words dull. Do not speak in euphemisms. Speak the truth, that it may cut the air of this wretched night. Your visions are visions of conspiracy, self-interest, and bloody murder, not tragedy or destiny, but the games of men. And do not pity those who die, have died, for they are victims of nature, not destiny. Stories, statistics, something less than human.

Show some compassion. Some of them are our friends.

No, every time you tell this tale, they become components of a story. If I call it a massacre, they become reduced to a word, a metaphor. If the future is already told, how can they still be people? How can we feel compassion for something that has been reduced to a word, a sentence, a twist in the tale?

You can be so harsh.

The only thing I care about, can care about, is murder, a crime of jealousy. Call me hypocritical, but it is our son, my son, and only in this case are we fit to speak, but even here, your words are stale. You skirt around the issue. Your dreams unmask a jealous king, but you daren't say it.

Shush. Someone could be listening.

You and your eavesdroppers again.

I just fear for my life. It's only natural.

Oh my husband's left me for cowardice.

They will not take kindly to threats. We must be careful with our words.

Wasn't it Confucius who insisted on the rectification of names?

He hasn't reached these shores, I'm afraid, hasn't been translated.

Nevertheless, he would hang his head in shame to see you tiptoeing around your intent. Call a spade a spade. Speak or forever hold your peace.

Aren't you scared?

Of course I am. I'm terrified. I am possessed by a consciousness that is nothing without doubt. Yet a word is little more than a noise if it strays from what's real and true.

Shush. I will not risk the ire of the king.

There is no king here, not in this deep, dark night, just a frigid silence and the terrible peace.

It's so dark, I can't see a thing. Shall we light a lamp?

No, I can't bear for you to see me now.

It's not as though I'm doing any better. A hollow creature, an empty shadow, staring at your quivering and frightened shape. Nothing but a mirror. True, I can't stand to look at you. Perhaps I should go outside.

How do we even know that there is a world out there? The darkness pens us within these walls, a universe unto itself.

I wonder what's outside.

Perhaps the outside has ceased to exist. Nothing exists if it is not observed. We could turn this to our advantage. With no observation, the universe becomes a blank canvas. There is no obligation on our part, not to memory, not to permanence. There is no outside. Perhaps we can draw this reality anew, our last gambit to change what has been set in stone. We could rewrite everything, kings of infinite space.

But you know of the eyes and ears, the eavesdroppers. We are not sealed off from them.

Alas.

Somewhere somehow somewhen someone is listening in on us, reading our tale.

I suppose you're right.

Look, look outside. Nothing has changed. I know too well that you are correct. Reality is suspect. Yet, I am powerless despite its quantum uncertainty. What is it that tethers us to this world?

Change the subject. This is unbearable.

Do you remember the day that our boy was born?

Yes. How could I forget? He was born by the water on the fifth night of the fifth month, in the second year of the king's reign. His first cry pierced the cold air of the night, and under the moonlight, I saw a birthmark on his left wrist in the shape of a kidney. It's been seven years.

I can't bear to lose him. He mustn't go.

Keep your voice down. He overheard us the other day.

You didn't tell me.

I went out of the room and he was standing in the dark. He looked at me as though he knew that it was time, and that he wanted me to understand that it was time. I didn't say a word. I think I held my breath, afraid to fracture the tenuous silence, afraid to let the moment spill into the next, as though I could prolong our time together, as though I could stop the inevitability of fate. Yet, we both know that the visions imply certainty.

Look at us, pathetic figures, characters of some fable, metaphors for some story beyond the reach of our comprehension, ready to be analysed. Here we stand, barely father and mother, barely husband and wife, discussing the death of our child as a matter of course, accomplices of a sort. We should be ashamed of ourselves. We ought to be defiant, rebels, asserting our independence, claiming agency. Perhaps I should write of this moment, perhaps I should take ownership, tell my own tale.

What good is writing? It is a unique craft, in which traces of performance vanish, time becomes contracted, confused, jumbled and interrupted. You seek to leave a coherent trace. Writing leaves a jumbled shape.

And yet it most accurately depicts our reality, a tranquil surface concealing a greater chaos, its time out of joint, its implications like the secrets of the deep.

Only if you are perceptive to its illusions.

I have been thinking about these visions of yours. Perhaps you are right, that it has all already happened, since it must all surely draw from some pool of data. Their present is our history, or perhaps it is that we have emerged from a different moment.

Let's not contemplate this further. All this shoegazing won't get us anywhere. It just allows us to dally. Besides, if the future has already happened, then where is the sense in fighting it?

I suppose so. Yet, it feels right to be able to see your own history before you, to interact with it, to render violence upon its immaterial body. The fight may be futile, but the effort is all I seek, for it is its own meaning.

You're not making sense.

I've never asked: Do you have those dreams every night?

Almost, but of different things each night, related nonetheless. Some nights, I dream only of the creature, the sword of fate, a gleaming blade, quicksilver, swordfish, garfish, what does it matter, it's all the same, these things from the churning. It haunts me, this creature from the tyrant sea. Some nights I dream of the creature and nothing but the creature, and my mind shrinks and shrinks until all that it contains is the cold gleam of its skin, the tessellated scales, its impassive stare, each eye a perfect circle, much like the solemn moon, perhaps judging, or perhaps unable to pass judgement on our pathetic human games. They are expressionless, and in being so, they emphasise their exteriority to us, remaining so far outside of our language and our senses, so far removed from human comprehension, uniquely other. Sometimes, in the face of such strangeness, I feel myself being absorbed, subsumed, ingested into a greater purpose. And sometimes, my greatest fear is that I know that we too emerged from the sea, cut from the same cloth, flipping, flopping, gasping for air.

Did we emerge from it or did we abandon it?

It wasn't a conscious choice. There was so much more that could be found above the waves, and much less darkness. Or perhaps it was the sea that abandoned us, spitting us out from its rolling depths into the open, naked and slippery, cast out as in that old story about the garden. Perhaps it was the abyss that chose to remain unknown and unknowable. Perhaps its nature drove us mad.

Perhaps our ancestors saw the sun and reached for it.

Like Icarus, then. I wonder if this discussion is some kind of lesson, some sign telling us that we mustn't overreach. This is the vision prescribed to us. We shouldn't presume to know otherwise. We should know our stations, perform our roles. We mustn't know what we shouldn't know.

What are we to do if we already know what we mustn't?

The weight and the responsibility are ours to bear. We must adhere, or there will be no end to this slaughter, our daily reality, the violence that comes in waves, time and again, day after day, hour after hour, now red, now rust, now darkest poison. Does this not grate on your conscience in the slightest?

Don't you dare. My heart bleeds like yours, but surely you know that in choosing one scenario over the other, the weight of our consciences does not diminish, not least because we already know our sins. Perhaps the future is typically unknown so that we do not have to feel the guilt of our choices.

This I don't understand. There is no choice, and hence there cannot be guilt. And yet I feel it all the same, as though my place here in this time and place, each limb, each breath, every atom that comprises my material self, is to blame. And now, the violence of incomprehension and the incomprehension of violence, a minor quandary, but a quandary nonetheless. But let's be logical. Surely you understand that you enable a catastrophe in order to prevent a minor tragedy. Cast violence aside, woman. This is not about your son any longer.

Understand this: I am not the sentimental one here. I see fear in your face, the terrifying visage of a terrified man. Is there no part of you that yearns for agency? Don't you also feel like a puppet on a string? Indeed, I tempt violence, but of a metaphysical sort. I seek usurpation.

We must live up to our fates. I will go to him now. I will send him on his way.

No, come back.

I'm afraid this dialogue is over.

It wasn't much of a dialogue in the first place, just two sorry shadows grovelling in the dark.

Say what you will.

I will fetch him and keep him here.

No, he must go on his way. The dreams must mean something.

I—Our son has already gone. We... We are too late.

...Perhaps it's for the better.

His lamp is cold. It smells of soot. It hasn't been lit tonight. The room too is cold, devoid of the heat of the body, the warmth of the breath, not even a ghost. I must go and find him.

Woman, please.

Leave me alone. At least tonight. Let me go where I will. The palace is three hours away on foot. You know that I will not catch him, but I must walk nonetheless. Dawn is breaking. He has probably already seen the king, that jealous man, that childish tyrant.

Please! I will leave you now. The eavesdroppers, they're closing in. We've said too much. He will not take kindly to your vulgar speech.

Then go, cower and cringe, back into darkness. It's too late now. The cogs have turned, the jigsaw fallen into place. I will no longer know peace. I go as far as my legs will carry me, far enough away from the voices, but not far enough from the quiet world. Time is out of order, the future fixed, the soil stained, caked in your blood.

Day is breaking. It is cold outside. The wind still carries the sound of your voice, but it is an echo, displaced data from a different time and place, for you are no longer of this world, of your own volition. It seems the choice was not ours to make in the first place. My son, my son, I fear I cannot let you go, or perhaps I fear that I must.

I feel the sand encrusted on my feet, the grains between my toes. The morning air nips at my fingertips. I walk into the water, the waves coldly lapping at my heels. Yet, I cannot drown, nor will there be violence. Nothing avails me. Until my last days, I will be a revenant, walking the false reality of the earth, seeking to return to my former shape.

In my mind, I summon an image of your face and pretend that it is you. I hear the familiar trembling and the squeaks in your young voice. I watch as your eyes blink. And slowly, I see you vanishing from my sight, fading, disappearing, into nothing, a blank, no clue, no trace, not even the faintest impression, like art that exists in its own time, a burning brightness that fades into ash, into carbon, no excess.

The perfect performance.

It leaves only the memory of what once was, the echo. You were only a squall, a shadow, and I an accomplice to your perfect crime. Slowly the thought of you expands into the vast and shallow space of a story, growing in magnitude but becoming dilute. This is how you will be remembered, this is how you have chosen to be remembered. And one day you will be named anew, but by then, you will already have gone. We will all have gone. Nothing remains.

My son, I write your name in the sand, embracing the turning of the tide, embracing the soft decay of time, according to your wishes, letting the water take you away

letting the earth claim you.

As stars die, leaving spectres

to inhabit the sky

The lamps burn out, leaving

heat without flame

I write your name in the sand

no one will see or hear it again

know it again

except the waves

cinders

only cinders

■ NOTES

All photographs in this volume are mine or family photos.

The epigraph for this book is from:

Euripides, "Herakles", in *Grief Lessons: Four Plays by Euripides*, trans. Anne Carson (New York: New York Review Books, 2006), 38.

Entanglements

1. Enrique Vila-Matas, *Never Any End to Paris*, trans. Anne McLean (London: Vintage, 2014), 194.

2. T.S. Eliot, "Ash-Wednesday", in *Selected Poems of T. S. Eliot* (London: Faber and Faber, 2002), 73.

3. Zbigniew Herbert, "Time", trans. Alissa Valles in Zbigniew Herbert, *The Collected Poems: 1956–1998* (New York: HarperCollins, 2007), 558.

Triptych

1. Franz Kafka, "The Watchman", from Franz Kafka, *The Collected Stories*, trans. Willa and Edwin Muir, ed. Gabriel Josipovici (London: Everyman's Library, 1993), 396.

Gravity

1. *Blade Runner*, dir. Ridley Scott (Warner Bros., 1982).

Solaris

One: Interloper

The epigraph for this section is from:

Yu Xuanji, "The Fragrance of Orchids", in *The Clouds Float North: The Complete Poems of Yu Xuanji*, trans. David Young and Jiann I. Lin (Hanover: Wesleyan University Press, 1998), 3.

Image captioned "Giuseppe Arcimboldo, *Spring*. 1563" is credited to PAINTING / Alamy Stock Photo.

1. Julio Cortázar, *Hopscotch*, trans. Gregory Rabassa (New York: Pantheon, 1966), 95.

2. André Bazin, "The Ontology of the Photographic Image", trans. Hugh Gray in André Bazin, *What is Cinema?: Volume I* (Oakland: University of California Press, 2005), 13.

3. "Je est un autre." Arthur Rimbaud in a letter to Georges Izambard, dated 13 May 1871.

4. Zeami Motokiyo, "Fūshikaden", in Zeami Motokiyo, *On the Art of the Nō Drama: The Major Treatises of Zeami*, trans. J. Thomas Rimer and Yamazaki Masakazu (Princeton: Princeton University Press, 1984), 60.

Solaris

Two: The Hall of Echoes

Image captioned "Giuseppe Arcimboldo, *Four Seasons in One*

Head. 1590" is credited to VTR / Alamy Stock Photo.

1. Henry Ridley, "New and Noteworthy Plants", *The Gardeners' Chronicles*, 24 June 1893, 740. A transcript is available at https://www.biodiversitylibrary.org/item/256482#page/1/mode/1up.

2. Julio Cortázar, *Hopscotch*, trans. Gregory Rabassa (New York: Pantheon, 1966), 165.

3. Roland Barthes, "Arcimboldo, or Magician and Rhétoriqueur", in Roland Barthes, *The Responsibility of Forms: Critical Essays on Music, Art, and Representation*, trans. Richard Howard (New York: Hill and Wang, 1985), 146.

4. Jacques Derrida, "The Taste of Tears", trans. Pascale-Anne Brault and Michael Naas, in Jacques Derrida, *The Work of Mourning*, ed. Pascale-Anne Brault and Michael Naas (Chicago: The University of Chicago Press, 2001), 110.

Solaris

Three: Dispatches

1. Jacques Derrida, *The Post Card: From Socrates to Freud and Beyond*, trans. Alan Bass (Chicago: University of Chicago Press, 1987), 11.

2. Julio Cortázar, *Hopscotch*, trans. Gregory Rabassa (New York: Pantheon, 1966), 7.

3. Paul Valéry, "A B C", in *Paul Valéry: An Anthology*, ed. James R. Lawler (Abingdon: Routledge & Kegan Paul, 1977), 174.

Ghost Stories

1. Giorgio Agamben, "Of the Uses and Disadvantages of Living among Specters", trans. David Kishik and Stefan Pedatella, in *The Spectralities Reader: Ghosts and Haunting in Contemporary Cultural Theory*, ed. María del Pilar Blanco and Esther Peeren (London: Bloomsbury Academic, 2013), 474.

2. Jacques Derrida and Bernard Stiegler, *Echographies of Television: Filmed Interviews*, trans. Jennifer Barojek (Cambridge: Polity Press, 2002), 120.

Metamorphoses (II)

1. José Ángel Valente, "Consent", in José Ángel Valente, *Landscape with Yellow Birds*, trans. Thomas Christensen (Brooklyn: Archipelago Books, 2013), 11.

Cinders

The epigraph for this section is from:
Jacques Derrida, *Cinders*, trans. Ned Lukacher (Minnesota: University of Minnesota Press, 2014), 48.

1. Alastair Reid, "Neruda and Borges", *The New Yorker*, 16 June 1996, 72.

■ ACKNOWLEDGEMENTS

The existence of this book owes much to Parker Smith, whose attentive reading and thoughtful suggestions helped to organise the ideas and restructure the text. Most of all, without his belief in the project, it would probably have never come into being.

I am grateful to Daryl Lim for his editorial insight in helping to shepherd this book to its current form.

I am also indebted to the many people who have supported this project in one way or another, too numerous to name, but a few of them are: Adrianne, Hao Guang, Yang, Matt, Casidhe, Nicholas, Chang Yin, Wei Fen, Rose, Stephanie, Jonathan, Mike, Xiao Yun, Yuming, Natalie, and Kah Wee.

"Triptych" was originally published in *Quarterly Literary Review Singapore* 13.4.

"Solaris" was developed from a manuscript produced during a National Arts Council (Singapore) writing residency programme in 2015 at the Singapore Botanic Gardens. I am grateful to everyone who supported my work during the residency, particularly Dr Nigel Taylor, Elango, and David.

A version of "Metamorphoses (II)" was longlisted for the *Australian*

Book Review Calibre Essay Prize in 2018.

The original version of "Ghost Stories" (as "Ghost") was longlisted for the *Australian Book Review* Elizabeth Jolley Short Story Prize in 2021.

About the Author

Daryl Li is a writer of fiction and nonfiction whose work has appeared in publications such as *OF ZOOS*, *Quarterly Literary Review Singapore*, *NANG*, and *Gastronomica*. *The Inventors* is his debut collection. He was born and raised in Singapore, where he is currently based.

ROSETTA
CULTURES

About Rosetta Cultures

Rosetta Cultures is an imprint by TrendLit Publishing that focuses on championing and bridging languages and the arts across cultures and communities.

Rosetta Cultures is currently based in Singapore, serving local and international readers.

National Library Board, Singapore Cataloguing in Publication Data
Name(s): Li, Daryl.
Title: The inventors / Daryl Li.
Description: [Singapore] : Rosetta Cultures, 2023.
Identifier(s): ISBN 978-981-18-8244-9 (paperback)
Subject(s): LCSH: Self--Literary collections. | Reminiscing--Literary
collections. | Memory--Literary collections.
Classification: DDC S828--dc23

Rosetta Cultures, an imprint by TrendLit Publishing Private Limited

37 Tannery Lane, #06-09, Tannery House, Singapore 347790

+65 6980 5638

contact@trendlitpublishing.com

www.seabreezebooks.com.sg

The Inventors

Editor(s) | Daryl Lim, Ang Jin Yong
Designer | Tan Boon Hui